Gagzy, Gogzy, and the Secret Isl[...]

The Defence of Eilean

Book Five: The Escapades of Gagzy and Gogzy

If you like this book, please leave a comment on my Facebook page - "Elisabeth promoting new author James Rae." or my TikTok page - "The Gagzy and Gogzy series."

Trial / Test Copy.

Rae.

Disclaimer

For parental guidance, this story has passages dealing with hauntings and ghosts. The story also alludes to medieval punishments.

Author's note

Before you read the story of Gagzy, Gogzy, and the secret island, there is a challenge.

So, take two round coins, the same size, and draw, tightly, a circle around one.

Now there is a question:

Can both those coins, and no other object, be put inside the circle without them touching each other?

The answer is *'no, they can't'*.

If they're in the circle with nothing between them, then they must be touching. That is certain. One must be on top of the other.

Now there is another challenge.

Take a pair of your own shoes and place them on the floor.

Look at them. What do you see?

You see, of course, a pair of your own shoes.

Now there is a second question:

If a ghost is there with you, can it place its two ghostly feet inside your shoes, as you do the same, without the two pairs of feet touching each other?

The answer is *'yes it can'*, because it's a ghost, and unlike the two coins, it isn't solid.

A ghost has no bones or muscles, and so it has no weight.

That ghost can stand inside your shoes just as you stand there, without you even knowing it.

Unless…

Unless you have the rare gift of the *'sight'*.

In that case, you would **see** the ghost as you put your own feet into your shoes.

But even if you don't have the *'sight'*, and the ghost is friendly, you might still sense the warm presence of that friendly ghost.

Now, take your feet out of your shoes, step back, and stare hard at those shoes.

Is the friendly ghost still standing there, wearing them?

In the story which follows, sisters, Gagzy and Gogzy, discover an invisible island, in the **same** place as a Scottish island in the Atlantic Ocean.

Those two islands are together in that same place, one seen and one unseen, in the same way as you and the friendly ghost, stood together in your shoes.

The invisible island is Eilean, and the Scottish island is Moreau Island.

Eilean is the home of other-worldly beings who need the help of Gagzy and Gogzy.

They need their help because the two sisters have the rare gift of being psychic. They have the *'sight'*.

They become partners in defence of the island of Eilean.

A Visit to the Library

It was three weeks into the summer holidays from school.

Gagzy and Gogzy, sat in their secret hideaway, the treehouse, which was hidden among branches of a giant beech tree in their back garden.

"What's a dimension, Gogzy? Do you know?"

Gagzy was three years older than Gogzy who was very smart.

"I know what it is, Gagzy. It's height, length or depth, the dimensions of our world. Or… Well… It's like, our world is our dimension."

"Do you think there are other worlds in other dimensions, Gogzy?"

"Well, we kind of know there are, don't we, because we've been in the Kingdom of the Fae."

"I suppose. Ok, so, our world is our dimension… But here's another question… What's a mystery?"

"Heh! That's a hard one! But I'll take a guess at answering it. It's like an impossible riddle or… Maybe it's a ghost.

Yes, a ghost is a mystery."

"But why? Why is a ghost a mystery?"

"Well, because a ghost isn't like us. It doesn't weigh anything. Remember when we met Penny on Moreau Island. She was a ghost. We could see her, but if we touched her… She wasn't there! That's a mystery, Gagzy."

Gagzy was Gabriella, and Gogzy was Gloria, but they preferred to be known by their nicknames.

They were reading the local newspaper and chatting about Moreau Island, the small, unpopulated island near their home, off the west coast of the Scottish mainland. It was known as Moreau Island, after its last owner, Pierre Moreau, in the seventeenth century.

The sisters shared a unique bond. They were psychic, a gift given to them by the timing of their births. They were bonded in mystical time…

So, they were born in mysterious time, both having come into the world at 7 minutes and seven seconds past 7 o'clock in the morning of the 7th day of the 7th month of July, and three years apart.

The timing of their births was the same, to exactly one single second.

Gagzy was eleven and Gogzy was eight years old.

They looked alike, both having long, shiny, red hair and sparkling blue eyes.

Gagzy was about four inches taller. She was daring and adventurous. She took risks, instead of stopping to think before she rushed into a challenge. And she did daft things like, sometimes making up her own words instead of sticking to the ones in the dictionary.

Her favourite subject was nature, and everything about plants and animals.

Gogzy was the opposite, cautious and scared of taking risks, often reminding her older sister, *'look before you leap'* and *'Don't rush in.'*

Gogzy had courage but she could become very worried if something scary came along. Being the smarter of the two, she received great school reports. And she knew lots of things, because she read all kinds of books.

Gogzy didn't invent new words of her own and often told Gagzy to stop doing that.

They sat in the treehouse and Gagzy was shocked at what she saw in the newspaper.

"Look at this, Gogzy, look what it says!"

An ancient fourteenth century skeleton with no feet has been found buried in castle ruins on Moreau Island.

"Yikes!", exclaimed Gogzy.

"Why would someone be buried with no feet? What else does it say?"

"It says some people have bought Moreau Island and they want to build things there.

They were digging when they found this very old skeleton near the castle ruins… But why did it have no feet?

It says…"

Gagzy paused, looking for the reason the skeleton had no feet.

"It says that long ago the castle had a prison hidden in its dungeons, and if anyone was caught trying to escape, they were punished by having their feet chopped off, so they couldn't try to run away again."

"Yikes, yikes, yikes! Yikes three times! That is not fair!", exclaimed Gogzy.

"That's a bit too much! Couldn't they just tie their legs together, Gagzy. Thank goodness they don't do stuff like that anymore."

"I know, Gogzy, but listen, I want to go back and visit the castle ruins and see what's going on over there."

"Does it say any more in the newspaper, Gagzy?"

"All it says is… They'll be building things. And that people can still visit the island for day trips.

So, I think we should go back today. We've never explored the castle ruins. We've seen them from a distance, but never from close. I would like to scout around the big, tumbled-down stones and the bits of building that are still standing. And there's the river that runs down the hillside beside the ruins. I want to see what plants and trees are growing there, and the birds and all. There's bound to be lots of animals too, because no one lives on the island. Wild animals love it when humans aren't there.

I just hope the people who found the skeleton aren't scaring the animals."

"But Gagzy, I'm not sure about going back right now. They shouldn't be digging up skeletons. They might wake up the ghosts. People say Moreau Island is a haunted island."

"Gogzy, I know what you're like, so don't start getting spooked. Remember, we know a little about ghosts.

So, we know not all ghosts are bad guys. Remember the golden rule… Ghosts might be spooky, making weird noises and banging things, but they can't harm people who are alive, ok."

"I suppose so, Gagzy."

"So, let's take the short boat trip later today, and do a wee bit of snooping around the castle ruins."

"But wait, Gagzy… It's true, we know not all ghosts are bad guys, but we don't know anything about the ones who **are** bad guys! And that's why I'm not sure about them. I mean it's not like they're alive, like all the Fae people. Those Fae people we've met… They're just as alive as we are… Pixies, faeries, Gnomes, nymphs and all the others, they're alive like us.

But ghosts… They're different… They're meant to be dead!

That's why I'm worried about being around them, just in case they're mean and nasty… Just in case they're unfriendly.

So, Gagzy, I want to pay a visit to the library first. I'm sure there's a book about the castle and its ruins.

That poor skeleton was buried 700 years ago. I want to know more about the castle at that time, before we go."

"Ok, Gogzy. I suppose if we read about things that were happening way back then, it won't seem so scary.

We could spend maybe an hour reading the book, then catch the visitor's boat at 1.00 o'clock. How about that?"

"Ok, Gagzy. Reading the book will give us a clue about what it was like to live there long ago.

And don't forget the ancient rumours that are still around today, that Moreau castle **is** one of the most haunted castles in Scotland.

Even though it's in ruins now, I just want to be prepared, and reading a book is a good way to do that."

"Yes.", Gagzy agreed.

Gogzy had made up her mind. If there were ghosts, she wanted to be ready for them.

They arrived at the library, and finding the book in the Scottish history section, they looked for a reading table. But before she even sat down, Gogzy was already in a bit of a panic.

"Gagzy look at the title on the cover of the book. It says in big black letters:

The Castle of Terror and Torment.

"Don't get too jumpy, Gogzy. Let's just see what it says inside. And remember, it's telling us about long ago. It's not talking about now, 700 years later."

Gogzy opened the book and read the opening lines aloud.

"The castle had a prison, a dungeon for bad guys. Escape would not have been easy, as the sea around it was deep and choppy."

"What else does it say?"

"Ok, it starts talking about how it was a place of terror and torment, and that even to this day, many wraiths and phantoms are believed to haunt the castle ruins.

Oh no! Why are we even **thinking** of going there, Gagzy?"

"What are wraiths, Gogzy?", Gagzy tried to change the subject.

"It's just something like a ghost or a spirit. And there might be lots of them in among the castle ruins! That's what it's saying!", Gogzy squealed.

"Let's not get spooked too quickly, Gogzy. I told you the golden rule… They can't harm people who are alive. So, tell me more about what's in the book. You read and I'll listen."

Gagzy wasn't easily spooked.

Gogzy was, and she answered, squeakily:

"Ok, I'll do my best. So, it says…

The island had a scary reputation, and because of its dungeons, the castle was said to be haunted.

But no one is sure about this now. It's probably just rumours… Like the one about a phantom gaoler who swings a chain with a spiky ball and brandishes a mighty sword. He was the boss of the prison and the one in charge of punishing people. He chopped off the feet!"

Gogzy gulped as she said those words about the phantom gaoler.

Gagzy didn't gulp.

"Gogzy… This book is saying a lot of the scary talk is just rumours… People making up stories."

"But what about that phantom gaoler, Gagzy. What if it **is** still in the castle ruins, swinging a ball and chain and a mighty sword? What if he tried to chop off **our** feet! Yikes!" Gogzy yelped at the thought of it!

"Gogzy, just think of what I keep telling you. Ghosts can't harm us humans.

And isn't a phantom gaoler just a shadowy shape?

Isn't his mighty sword just the same? A phantom sword can't chop off anything.

So, what else does the book say?"

"Oh, no! I can't read this bit, Gagzy, here it is… you read it."

"Ok, but calm down. Let me see… It's telling us the castle was built with a prison to lock up traitors, spies, and thieves. And it's saying only the worst of the bad guys were kept there. It says anyone who tried to escape would have their feet chopped off, so, they could never run away again. That's what happened to our skeleton, Gogzy, the one in the newspaper. What a fate! And oh… I get it Gogzy, these must be the bits you didn't want to read."

Gogzy covered her ears.

This was a terrible place. It wasn't just feet that were chopped off. Anyone caught stealing food from the prison kitchen would have their hands chopped off. There are tales of hands which can be seen to this very day, floating, with no arms and sometimes making clapping sounds.

Gagzy interrupted her reading.

"Gogzy, that's just a daft story about hands that might be clapping. It's a story made up by people who like to spread gossip. Surely, you can see that."

"Ok, Gagzy, just finish reading then we can go home."

"Ok.", Gagzy continued.

"One legend remains, of a headless horseman who, after his head was chopped off, his legs were still working, and he jumped on his horse and escaped. Visitors to the island still claim to have seen the horse and its headless rider jumping over the castle moat to escape.

But here's the good bit, Gogzy.

While such stories are interesting, they should not be taken too seriously, for one very good reason.

Nowadays everyone carries a phone with a camera, and no picture has ever been taken of a floating pair of clapping hands, a ghost with no feet, or a horseman with no head.

It's saying all the scary stuff is just rumours.

So, don't be scared by talk of ghosts and missing body bits. Let's talk to mum, she doesn't believe in ghosts anyway. So, if she says it's ok to go, we can get the 1.00 o'clock crossing. I'm keen to see those castle ruins. Will you do that?"

"Ok, but **we** know ghosts are real because we've met one before. She was Penny, and she even became our friend.

But I'll remember the golden rule, just in case we meet a nasty one… **Ghosts can't harm us humans**.

And if we see one, I need to remember that it's not truly there. It just looks like it's there. I'll try hard to remember that."

"Well said, Gogzy."

A Lady with Glossy, Red Lipstick and a Mysterious Meeting

The sisters set off wearing denim jackets, blue jeans, and luminous, flashing blue trainers.

The small boat crossed the water in just a few minutes.

Only a few people were on it.

"Gagzy…". Gogzy whispered in her sister's ear.

"Why is that lady staring at us?"

"Which one, Gogzy?", Gagzy whispered back.

"The one with the glossy, red lipstick. She looks angry."

"I'll ask her, Gogzy…"

Gagzy wasn't shy. She would jump in if she wanted an answer.

"Excuse me, have we met you before?", she asked politely.

The lady answered in a way that wasn't polite.

"I know you two.", she said in a growly voice.

"You're the two redheads, who talk about magic and ghosts, and all that stuff that scares other kids. I've heard everything about you. So, what's your business on Moreau Island? I'm one of the new owners of the island and I like to know who's coming and going. What's your business over there."

"We like to visit during our summer holidays. Our dad's a policeman, and he says its ok to visit. And so does the newspaper." Gagzy answered, not scared off by the angry voice of the lady with the glossy, red lipstick.

"You can visit.", the lady replied.

"But if I hear any talk about ogres, goblins or Gnomes with hairy feet, I'll come looking for you two. We're starting a business on the island, and we don't want customers and visitors to be scared off by scary stories. Do you hear what I'm saying?"

"We hear.", Gagzy answered as the boat steered into the jetty.

But the lady with the glossy, red lipstick hadn't finished.

She moved closer and whispered. She didn't want her friends to hear.

"So, tell me, how do you know about goblins, ogres, faeries and all the rest of them. How do you know about them? Tell me. I want to know more. Are they real? Are they? Are they?" Her whisper turned to a sharp squeak."

"Or do you make it all up to scare the other kids? Do you?", she snarled, whispering again.

"We don't make it up.", Gogzy answered, bravely.

"We just see what we see."

"And how do you see what you see? I want to see stuff like that. I want to know if it's real."

The lady wanted an answer.

"You have to have the gift." Gagzy answered.

"It's not something you can learn."

She was unhappy with Gagzy's answer. She didn't change her angry voice.

"Just you remember what I said. I'll be looking for you if you cause me any trouble."

After alighting from the boat, that lady with glossy, red lipstick and four others walked off in the direction of the castle ruins.

Gagzy and Gogzy followed, keeping their distance behind them.

"She wasn't very nice, talking to us like that, Gagzy."

"I know, she was nasty. I hope we don't see her again. But it wasn't just her island business she was worried about. It was more than that. She wanted to know how we're able to see the Fae people. She was nosy about that… Like she wished she could see them. Let's stop here for a while till she's out of sight."

They sat on the beach which soon became deserted.

Gagzy took off her jacket and pulled her long red hair into a ponytail at the back, and Gogzy, seeing the side of her sister's arm, asked about her tattoo.

"I love your tattoo, Gagzy. I wish mum would let me have one."

"It's only a small one, that's why she let me have it. It's the Celtic Tree of Life, the Oak tree.

Maybe mum will let you have one next year.

Will I fix you a ponytail at the back, Gogzy. It's quite blowy in the wind."

"No thanks, I like the feel of my hair blowing in the wind. I love the wind in summertime, Gagzy.

But listen, I've been thinking about the last time we were here on the island. I had a feeling we were being watched by someone. It was so strong a feeling, I was certain we were being watched."

"Me too, Gogzy… I had the same feeling. And I thought, whatever, or whoever was watching us, it wasn't invisible, it was just hiding.

I felt sure it was hiding. I could almost feel its eyes peeping at me, maybe from behind a bush or a tree, wondering who I was."

"Yes, and whatever it was, it must have known we have the *'sight',* the gift of seeing invisible people.

So, to spy on us… If it knew we could see invisible people, it decided it would hide, not knowing we can still sense when we're being watched."

"You're right, Gogzy. What do you think? Do you think we'll be watched when we go up the hill to the ruins? Do you think we might still be watched? Maybe they'll come and talk to us, whoever they are."

"Yes, maybe they'll show themselves this time.

Gagzy…"

Suddenly Gogzy's voice turned to a soft whisper into her sister's ear.

"Look over there, near the cliffside where the waterfall runs into the river. Do you see what I see… Those three girls sitting on the sand. Are they watchers? I've never seen anyone who looks like they do."

"Whow!" exclaimed Gagzy, also in a whisper.

"They are strange. They're girls. But one of them looks like a ghost! And the other two… They look so different from most girls. Let's go over and see if they'll talk to us."

"Are you sure? I mean are you sure we should go near them if one is a ghost?"

"Yes. We usually know if people are nasty or scary. They're friendly, I'm sure of it. Come on."

The sisters walked towards the mysterious trio.

"Hi, we're just visiting the island. I'm Gagzy, and this is my sister, Gogzy. Do you live here?"

The three figures who greeted them were astonishing.

The first to speak was garlanded with flowers and she had an aura all around her which glowed. She answered Gagzy's question.

"We three are elemental spirits, feminine spirits of three Forces of Nature.

I am Querciabella, an elemental spirit of the Earth."

Querciabella was dressed in the deep green colours of nature, with leaves quivering gently on her dress, and in one hand she held a glowing tree branch.

"I exist in two dimensions. One is Eilean, the other is Earth.", she told them.

"As an elemental spirit of Eilean, I have the *'sight'* of both Eilean and Earth.

In Eilean I may be seen only by humans who have the *'sight'* of other dimensions.

As a Force of Nature, I'm the oak tree Of Moreau Island. The Tree of Life is my earthly dimension, and I can be seen and touched by all in your world.

You are two sisters who have the *'sight'* of other dimensions so, you may see and speak with me, but you may not touch me, Gagzy and Gogzy.

I come to reveal to you a mystery. And it is this…

Change may beget change in another dimension."

The sisters gasped in wonder at Querciabella.

How did she know their names? And what was this mystery?

She spoke again to introduce a second feminine spirit of Eilean.

"This is my friend, Whitewave. She also exists in two dimensions. As an elemental, she is a spirit of the river and sea of Eilean. As a Force of Nature, she **is** the river and sea of Moreau Island."

Whitewave stood upright to show herself as a girl cloaked in long, white hair, her own hair, which hung all the way down to her knees.

"You are surprised we know your names, Gagzy and Gogzy, but I have the power of *'foresight'*, the vision of that which is yet to come, and I foresaw your arrival. We are here to meet you for the first time, but we will see you again soon.

You may see and speak with me as a spirit, but you cannot touch me. Such contact is impossible.

As a Force of Nature, you may touch me as water in my river or sea.

I also come to reveal to you a mystery, and it is this… **Change to my river and sea may beget change in another dimension.**

Now I will introduce you to Anemone, a daughter of the wind, and the third feminine spirit in our group. She also exists in two dimensions. As an elemental, she is a spirit of the wind of Eilean. As a Force of Nature, she is an earthly breeze or a turbulent storm… She is as she chooses to be."

Anemone was by far the strangest of the three mysterious figures.

She stood before them, ghostlike, seeming more of an outline than a body. She was like a silhouette, and when she spoke, her voice breathed the words, sometimes whispering, whistling and sometimes rustling.

"It is my privilege to see and speak with you across the dimensions. I am the elemental spirit of the wind of Eilean. You may speak with me, but you will see little of me. And you may not touch me. We are in different dimensions.

But if I blow strong, as a Force of Nature you may feel the power of the wind on your face.

I also come to reveal to you a mystery, and it is this…

The wind blows as it will, in any dimension."

"It's a privilege for us too…" Gagzy answered, awestruck by the whispering voice of Anemone.

"To talk to the wind… It's just amazing!", exclaimed Gogzy, feeling the soft blow of a breeze on her cheeks, as it whispered gently in her ears and rustled through her billowing hair.

"And you will see us again, soon."

Querciabella repeated Whitewave's words, and as she did so, all three vanished, leaving Gagzy and Gogzy entranced and alone on the beach.

They were psychic sisters, but they had never seen or spoken before to the three feminine Forces of Nature.

"Wow! They've skedaddled!", exclaimed Gagzy.

"They weren't watchers, Gogzy. Those guys were spirits, **and** Forces of Nature. Vanishing vapours! Holy smoke! Stunning stunners!"

Gagzy struggled to find the right words.

"What's this mystery about, Gagzy… Change in one dimension may beget change in another. And the wind blows as it will in any dimension. What does it mean? And why are they telling **us** about this mystery?"

"I don't know Gogzy. I don't even know what *'beget'* is? What does it mean?"

"I think it's just… If one thing begets another… Well, it kind of makes the other thing happen."

"Ok, Let's head up to the castle ruins, Gogzy. Maybe we'll learn more about this mystery later."

"Ok. We've never met Forces of Nature before. But aren't there four, not just three?"

"What's the fourth one?"

"Well, there's Earth, Wind, and Water… That's the three we just met. But I think the fourth one is Fire."

"I wonder what that one looks like, Gogzy."

"Yikes!", exclaimed Gogzy.

"I wonder if we can touch it! I hope not!"

Eilean

Moreau Island and Eilean were together, in the same point on the ocean, but as separate dimensions.

Earth, Air, Fire and Water were elemental beings within Eilean.

They had the *'sight'* of Earth and its natural world but were part of it only as Forces of Nature.

And they were not alone on Eilean. They shared that peaceful place with two races of the Fae … In one race were troupes of Pixies, in the other, three clans of Eilean Gnomes.

In Eilean, Pixies and Gnomes were invisible to most humans who might visit Moreau Island, but they were not invisible to the spirits of Earth, Air, Fire and Water.

The Pixies, Gnomes and those spirits of Earth, Air, Fire and Water… They had the *'sight'* of each other.

The Fae people had the *'sight'* of Querciabella.

If they needed help, she was their leader.

In her earthly form, Querciabella was the oak tree which withstood many storms as a young sapling … storms which gave her strength in later years.

The strength of the great Oak was Querciabella's own strength, coming from the tree's outstretched roots which spread upwards into branches and leaves, giving sturdy defences against the passing ravages of time.

She was a respected leader in Eilean.

When troubles arose, she revealed her strength. And she never gave up.

She remained as the Tree of Life remained… Strong and enduring.

She was a feminine elemental spirit, so, she appeared as a girl, but her living being, her true self… It was the life of the Oak tree, and not the life of any human.

She lived as the tree lived.

Whitewave and the Fae folk also had the *'sight'* of each other.

As a Force of Nature, she was the river and the sea of Moreau Island.

As an elemental spirit of Eilean, she loved its purifying power to heal and nurture life. She loved every flowing curve and bend of the river's journey to the sea.

Sometimes, she wept when seeing the suffering of animals who lived on the riverbanks. She felt their pain, and, when unable to contain her feelings, she dived into the deep sea of Eilean, to hide, alone with her thoughts.

Whitewave loved animals.

Birds and animals could see her but could not reach out and touch her. She was known to weep waves of sadness if she saw an injured rabbit or a bird in distress and was unable to help.

Whitewave's power of *'foresight'* could be a bringer of pain. Seeing future events before they happened was a gift which could be a great burden to the one who had that power.

To anyone with the *'eye"*, the *'sight'* to see her, she was a girl.

But her living being, her true self… was the life of river and sea, and not the life of any human being.

Anemone was also known to the Fae folk. She was a daughter of the wind, an elemental spirit of the air, ghostly and almost invisible.

To anyone with the *'sight'*, she could almost be seen as a girl, with a form so fine, she was as fine as light.

Her hair glowed as shimmering beams, a hazy silhouette, screening her graceful body.

As a Force of Nature, she was a soaring power, a stormy gale, or a gentle breeze.

She might gust as a gentle breeze, or cause havoc and chaos as a storm.

She could be angry and wild, or breezy and calm.

Unlike Whitewave, she could ignore the feelings of others. There were times when she chose to be a bringer of destruction.

Anemone was a baffling mystery, a changing wind which blew as she wished.

As an elemental she posed as a girl, but her true self was the erratic life of the wind and not that of any human being.

The mysterious Elemental spirit of Fire was also known to the Fae folk of Eilean.

He was Ignis, and the fourth of the Forces of Nature.

As an elemental, Ignis could be seen by any with the *'sight'*, and he assumed more than one shape.

As a spirit, he too, could not be touched.

As a Force of Nature, he **could** be touched.

He was a bringer of blazing fire which might cause great destruction with grassland wildfires, or volcanoes spewing molten lava across the landscape.

Whatever form his appearance showed, Ignis was a terrifying sight to any with the *'eye'* to see him.

But his true self was not that of any ghastly being, it was the life of the raging fire.

He was known to the Fae races of Eilean.

Those Gnomes and Pixies knew of his lair, the place where he lived in shadow, and they stayed clear of it.

Ignis was **not** a friend of Querciabella, Whitewave or Anemone.

They too avoided him.

The Castle Ruins

The sisters left the spot where they met the three mysterious girls and headed for the hill with Moreau Castle ruins at the top.

They walked beside the cliffs, the quickest way to the hillside.

"Look how the waterfalls have formed a river, Gagzy. Some streams run through a cave on the side of the hill."

"Yes, and the rest of the river runs round the bottom.

Let's have a closer look at it from the bottom, Gogzy."

They saw it was fast flowing, with rocks in places, jutting above the surface.

They stood for a moment, listening to the ripple of waves flowing and swerving, following a zigzagging path.

There was an old bridge.

Gagzy walked on it, a few paces. It creaked and squeaked, but it was safe as Gogzy followed and they stepped gingerly across to the other side.

From there they had a better view of the riverbanks. They saw how the river swerved and turned a few times before flowing faster and curving left towards woods in the distance, where it would eventually run down to the sea.

They stood close to plants and trees, and listened to the trill of birdsong, that sound of music only birds can make.

Gagzy was wowed by what she saw and heard.

"Wow, Gogzy. This is amazing.

There's willow, alder, silver birch, and rowan trees, all bursting out on both sides of the riverbanks. And the plants... I know most of them. Those creamy whitish ones are meadowsweet. You can smell them from here. Those heart-shaped yellow ones are marsh marigolds. And can you smell the water mint, Gogzy?"

"It's lovely, and fresh."

"And that bright one, stay away from that guy, Gogzy, that's hemlock. It is pure poisonous. I'm not joking, it's drop-dead poisonous.

And the birds and butterflies are everywhere. Those birds near the alder tree, those are siskins and goldfinches, and that little one swimming, with the brown feathers, that's a grebe. Look, it's just ducked under the water."

"Yikes!", exclaimed Gogzy.

"Something jumped onto that rock and off again, Gagzy."

"I saw it. It was an otter. Maybe there's a family nearby. This place is so special. No one lives on this island, so, I bet animals feel safe here, and plants boom and bloom beside this river. That's how it should be. I just hope those people who found the skeleton don't scare the animals."

Someone answered Gagzy's concerns.

"Perhaps they will disturb the spirit of the river, and those who dwell within its rhythmic flow."

A voice spoke in bubbly, gargling tones, seeming to be both near and far away.

The words seemed to flow, almost like the flow of the river, and they were friendly.

"Heh! Who said zat zing?", Gagzy invented a new phrase, as she often did when surprised.

"Beo i Sith.", the voice answered.

"Who's there?", Gagzy asked again.

"Gagzy, look into the water, beside the Rowan tree.", said Gogzy.

Gagzy looked to see a face, a face which spoke from below the surface!

"Beo i Sith.", she said again in rippling tones, without rising above the surface.

For a moment, the sisters stood gazing, stunned, like statues. Gogzy broke the silence.

"Excuse me, but what are those words you speak?

And what do they mean? And how can you speak under water?" She asked the face under the water.

A head with long, white hair popped up, into the fresh air.

With her head above water, she spoke without gargling, and the sisters recognised her at once. She was Whitewave.

"My words mean *'Long live peace,'* as the spirit of my river is to live in peace. And I told you we would meet again. My spirit resides here in my river. The river and sea are my home."

"But how can you speak under water, Whitewave?",

"When I speak, I need to breathe air.", Gogzy told her.

"I may speak in both air and water. I speak under water because water is my element. It is my home."

With those words she turned and swam, leaping and plunging like a playful dolphin, to and from either side of the river, followed by a white frothy spume, a huge white wave.

Then, in a final flourish, she sprung onto the riverbank to become the girl with long white hair cloaked around her whole body.

She stood beside the sisters.

"Remember, you may see and speak with me, but you cannot touch me."

All three sat on the grassy verge, and Gogzy saw a chance to ask a question.

"What did you mean, Whitewave when you told us you came to reveal a mystery?

You said: Change to a river may beget change in another dimension.

"You will come to know the meaning of those words, Gogzy, through events which are yet to come." Whitewave answered cryptically.

So, the sisters must await future events to know the meaning of the mystery.

Gagzy changed the subject.

"I thought you might be a mermaid under the waves, Whitewave.", said Gagzy.

"But you have legs like me and Gogzy."

"I do, in my elemental form.

Meeting you again delights me, Gagzy and Gogzy. I've been expecting you."

"You knew we were coming!", exclaimed Gogzy.

"I did. I told you I had the *'foresight'*."

"You see the future, Whitewave?", Gagzy paid close attention. How could that be?

"You know the future before it happens!" exclaimed Gogzy.

"Sometimes we get a clue about the future in our dreams, Whitewave. But we never know for sure how it will turn out."

"The future may be hidden behind the mist of time to come, Gogzy? Or it may be seen in advance by one who has the gift, the *'foresight'*.

I also have the gift of the divination of doom.", she told them, some sadness in her voice.

"And such a gift is a heavy burden to bear. I see troubled times which are still to come. But I may not share this knowledge with another. To share my foresight of a coming disaster is to ensure that it will happen.

If I know of a coming disaster, I may only tell another of a secret which might prevent it."

Gogzy was quick to ask another question.

"If something bad was going to happen, would you tell Gagzy and me about that secret?"

The sisters waited for an answer when suddenly a little goldfinch landed beside Whitewave where she sat on the grassy verge.

"It's a goldfinch.", said Gagzy.

"The black cap and its red face tell me it's a goldfinch, Gogzy. I think it has hurt its wing. The wing has collapsed where the yellow patch is."

Gagzy knew a lot about birds.

"This little bird seeks the healing power of the river flowing through my fingers.," said Whitewave, whispering.

With the palm of her hand, she cupped water from the flowing river and allowed it to drip gently through her fingers onto the injured wing, saying:

"Fly away my little friend.", and instantly, the goldfinch took flight to its nest in a tree.

And as it did so, Whitewave slid into the river with words which answered Gogzy's question about knowing the secret to stop a disaster.

"Goodbye, Gagzy and Gogzy, until we meet again, the answer to your question, Gogzy, is this:

Trouble lies ahead for the Forces of Nature and the Fae of Eilean. So, my secret advice to the human sisters who stand before me is this… You must seek the advice of another."

"What other?" They called out together.

Whitewave's head had slipped beneath the flow of the river. The words of her reply were muffled and gargled.

"Seek the advice of the mum."

The sisters heard the muffled words sounding through the ripple of the water.

"The mum!" They exclaimed together, as they saw the huge spume of a white wave follow her into the distance.

"But what can that mean, Gogzy?

The mum!' Who's the mum?", she called after Whitewave who zig-zagged round a bend of the river.

"What mum?", Gogzy yelled, but Whitewave was gone.

"Maybe that's the secret, Gagzy. Maybe there's a special *'mum'* somewhere… Maybe not… No, it can't be that. I think she must have meant our **own** mum.

Whitewave won't have a mum like we have a mum. She's a river. So, maybe she just didn't say it right.

I think she meant we should seek the advice of our own mum. Don't you, Gagzy?"

"I suppose so. Ok, so, we've to seek the advice of our own mum?"

"Yes, but we can't until we get home. But anyway, what would we say to mum? Would we tell her we met a girl you thought was a mermaid, but she was really a spirit, and a Force of Nature, all rolled into one. She could breathe in water as well as breathe in air. And she could even cure sick birds!

Should we tell mum she had the gift of the divination of doom… a scary, scary gift, Gagzy… a heavy burden to bear, she said.

It means she can see the future if something bad is going to happen, but **we** can help her if we ask mum's advice first. What would she say to us, Gagzy? What would mum say to us?"

Gogzy asked her sister this big question, as the pitch of her voice rose with every single word she spoke. She was very excitable.

"Ok, calm down Gogzy. She would think we were sticking our noses into magic stuff again, after we promised we wouldn't do it. And she wouldn't believe any of it. So, when we ask mum about it, we must be careful how we say it.

All we can do for now is remember why we're here. We came to look at the castle ruins. We'll talk about telling mum later, ok?"

"Ok, Gagzy."

They sat by the riverbank and talked.

"I did think she was a mermaid. Until she came out of the water."

"She's not a mermaid, Gagzy."

"So, what is she, I mean, really. What is she?"

"We should just believe her. She said she's a spirit and a Force of Nature, and the river is her home. We've never met a spirit like her before, but that's enough for me. And I liked her. She wasn't a ghost, and she wasn't a bad guy. She knows the future, and she said, *'until we meet again.'* So, we will see her again."

"She could swim like a dolphin and talk under water!", exclaimed Gagzy.

"And she fixed that wee goldfinch's wing with a few drops of river water! And what a cool name! Whitewave!", Gagzy was impressed, if a little bit confused about what was going on.

No sooner had Whitewave disappeared, there was another sudden event on the riverbank.

"Yikes! What was that? Did you see it, Gagzy. That wasn't a bird."

"I saw it Gogzy. It was too big for a bird, but it had wings too, small wings with no colour… A bit like the Pixies we saw in the Kingdom of the Fae. It had a big head. And it carried a bag on its shoulder. I'm sure it did. It landed beside the silver birch tree. And now it has vanished. I think it might have been a watcher, Gogzy. I do. It looked at us! Then, *swooooosh*… It disappeared. Did you see how it vanished, Gogzy?"

"I saw it. It disappeared like a burst bubble. It's probably behind the tree trunk. I have a feeling we'll see it again, Gagzy. Maybe that was its way of saying '*Hi!*' Maybe it's shy."

"Maybe. Ok, let's head up the hill and check out the castle ruins, before someone else gives us a fright!"

"Ok. But what should we do if that woman with the glossy, red lipstick is up there, Gagzy?"

"We don't have to talk to her. And anyway, dad said we're allowed to be here, and so did the newspaper."

Arriving at the hilltop, they stood on a flat surface where they were greeted by a messy scene of shambles, but there was no sign of the woman with the glossy, red lipstick or her friends.

Around the ruins was a dry ditch which once would have been the castle moat.

Blocks of broken stones filled some flat grassland, covered in moss and wildflowers. Huge slabs of castle stone were piled high where buildings and walls had fallen. There were remains of turrets and parapets.

The sharp thorns and bright yellow flowers of the gorse bush grew across the hilltop.

Two things stood out which caught the sisters' attention.

One was an awesome oak tree, resplendent with deep green leafage which whispered and rustled in the summer breeze.

Gagzy couldn't contain her reaction.

"Wow, Gogzy! What a place and what an oak tree! It's magnificent, just like the tattoo on my arm.

Is this maybe Querciabella's Tree of Life, right in the middle of all this ruin? It's just standing here, on the hilltop, whispering in the breeze. Wow!"

"It's not fair, Gagzy. You have your tattoo. I want the same tattoo."

"Ask mum when we get home. You can tell her about this tree. She might let you have it, Gogzy."

The second standout ruin was baffling.

"Look at that, Gagzy… Near the oak tree.

How did it get to be there, standing like that?"

Gogzy saw a round tower, pointed at the top. It was standing, but not upright. It was leaning.

Battered by storms for centuries, it was forced down, halfway to the ground, but still standing, like a big pencil, stuck at an angle, into the hilltop.

"We could run up its side wall, Gogzy. But I don't think we'll try. It might just collapse completely, and us with it!"

 "Look, Gagzy, it has a doorway at the bottom. It looks like a trapdoor, a hatch, leading underground but it's blocked by bushes."

"They're gorse bushes, Gogzy. We wouldn't get past them even if we wanted to. They have those jaggy thorns. They would cut our skin and tear our clothes. So, we won't be going down there. I bet it leads to the prison dungeons, the place where the ghosts are, and hands and feet were chopped off."

Gogzy shuddered at that thought.

"Don't remind me, Gagzy!"

"I don't know what this tower is, Gogzy?", said Gagzy.

"It's not the right shape for a house. I wonder if anyone lives there."

"Maybe it's a turret, Gagzy. Some had pointed tops, where guards watched for enemies, and strangers in the nighttime…

But surely, no one could live there now, even if they managed to get past the gorse bushes. Might someone still be living there? Surely not."

Gagzy didn't have time to answer.

Querciabella

Gagzy didn't have time to answer because a third voice came from the oak tree, one which spoke in soft, gentle tones, like Whitewave from the river.

"Beo i Sith." She said the same words as Whitewave, then she asked a question.

"Is a home a building? Or is it the spirit of the one who dwells within?"

"Who dat der?", Gagzy asked, making up some silly words as her eyes searched for the speaker.

They turned surprised, but no one was there until, mysteriously, a girl walked out of the trunk of the oak tree. No door opened. She just appeared from behind the bark, and the sisters saw at once who she was.

She was Querciabella.

"Yikes! It's you!", exclaimed Gogzy.

"How did you do that? And the words you said. We've heard them before."

"Tree trickery!", exclaimed Gagzy.

"Were you hiding behind the oak tree, Querciabella?", she asked.

In her hand she held the tree branch which glowed with a warm aura.

She smiled and answered the questions of both girls.

To Gogzy she said:

"The bark of the great oak doesn't bar me, and the words I spoke mean *'Long live peace.'*

It's the motto of Eilean."

And in answer to Gagzy's question she said:

"I didn't hide behind the great oak; I live within it. This tree is my home."

"Yikes!", exclaimed Gogzy.

"That's brill! We have a tree house too. We don't live in it. But we sometimes sleep in it during the summer months. It's a fun place in our back garden."

"That's a *'wow!'* dress you're wearing, Querciabella. I've never seen one like it.", said Gagzy, enchanted.

Querciabella stood in a glow of light and colour.

Her hair was a deep green hue, the colour of the oak tree's summer leaves, and festooned by a garland, multi-coloured with wildflowers, of blue-green, crimson, purple, red, and yellow.

Her knot-patterned earrings were fashioned from the finest branchlets.

More wildflowers adorned her ankles and wrists.

Her dress was banded at the waist, and covered in layers of natural leaf, the deep green shade of summer oakleaf.

Her eyes too, shone mysteriously, with a green intensity.

Her skin was the lightest green, and her arms and feet were bare.

Butterflies and woodland birds fluttered around her shoulders. Squirrels and rabbits played near her feet, but none of the birds or animals touched her.

"Your dress is so amazing.", Gogzy spoke again.

"It almost looks like it's alive!"

"My dress **is** alive, Gogzy. As is every part of me."

"Wow!", exclaimed Gagzy.

"You mean **every** part, like the wildflowers, the leaves, the earrings, they're all alive?"

"Yes, Gagzy. They live so long as I live. Even the band around my waist is alive. They have the life of my oak tree within them."

"And that branch in your hand, Querciabella, what's that? Is it alive?"

"Oh, I should have introduced her."

"Her!", the sisters exclaimed, almost in unison.

"Oh, yes, she is Cumhachd, and yes, she is alive. She comes to my aid in times of need. But mostly she is silent and peaceful."

"Wow! Cumhachd!", they exclaimed together, staring, in awe of Querciabella, and of Cumhachd.

Gagzy changed the subject.

"So, Querciabella, what's it like living inside an oak tree?

"And how come you have green hair?

Me and Gogzy, we're sisters. We're unusual because we both have red hair and blue eyes. But I don't think we've ever met anyone with green hair. Have we Gogzy?"

"Nope, I don't think so, Gagzy.", Gogzy answered, a little embarrassed by Gagzy's question.

Sometimes she could be cheeky without meaning to be cheeky.

Querciabella didn't answer right away.

"Before I answer your question, Gagzy, I will say again what I told you when we met beside the cliffs.

I see and hear you. But I may not touch you or any earthly being. We are in different dimensions.

But I'm different from the Pixies and Gnomes with whom we share Eilean. They have a portal into the human dimension. They may see, hear, and even touch, if they choose to do so, any human being with the *'sight'* to see them. Such gifted humans are rare in your world, Gagzy and Gogzy… You are among that rare few.

But I won't tell you what it's like inside my oak tree. I'll show you. Come inside, see my Eilean home, and I'll tell you why my hair is green."

Querciabella led the way towards the trunk of the tree. She touched its bark, and it glowed with a soft light, allowing the girls to walk through it.

They entered a large round room, much wider than the measure of the tree.

It was bright with three round windows, not seen from outside, flooding sunlight into the space.

There was much to see and sense.

Two armchairs with plump, soft green cushions sat on either side of an oak table, which seemed to be alive, with a bark covered top, and roots! It stood before the glowing embers of a fire at the base of an ivy-covered chimney.

"Wow!", Gagzy whispered in Gogzy's ear, excited by all she saw.

A cauldron sat on a smaller fire in a corner. Pots bubbled.

A rope ladder hung from a high ceiling. Were there more rooms above?

Curved shelving stacked with bottles, books, and potteries decked the sides of the circular walls.

Tables shaped like giant toadstools were placed beside chairs with legs which seemed to be rooted, growing out of the floor!

A large, round carpet covered the middle of the floor. It was embroidered with Celtic knotwork and showed the Tree of Life at its centre.

It brought another *'wow!'* from Gagzy as she took in the scene.

To any visitor seeing it for the first time, this treehouse was a place full of wonder and surprise.

"I'm gobsmacked!", Gagzy broke the silence.

"What a treehouse, Querciabella. I've never seen such a place!

I want to live here. It's unbescribable!"

Gagzy hadn't lost the habit of making up her own words when the occasion demanded it. Gogzy usually tried to stop her doing it.

"Stop it, Gagzy.", she told her sister abruptly.

"It's wonderful, Querciabella. You are so lucky to live in such a fabulous place.", she said excitedly.

"Would you like some herbal tea?" Querciabella asked.

"Yes, please." They answered together.

"Sit in one of the armchairs. They're big enough for two, and I'll bring the tea.

Querciabella came back with an aroma of mint tea in mugs with ornate designs on the sides.

"I bring you Eilean mint tea in cups of Eilean pottery. These are not objects of your world, Gagzy and Gogzy."

She placed the mugs on the table as Gagzy gasped in surprise, not at the cups, but at Querciabella's fingernails.

"Scratchy scrapers!", she exclaimed.

"Look at those nails, Gogzy."

"They're amazing.", said Gogzy, worried Gagzy was being cheeky again.

Querciabella's nails were long, sharp, and the same light green colour as her skin.

"Oh, yes... My fingernails. They are long and very sharp. Sharp fingernails can be useful."

"How would you use them?", Gagzy asked.

"Once in a while, a screaming howler may attempt to enter my home, the Tree of Life. When it does, I scratch, angrily, the inner bark of the trunk. If this doesn't deter the fiend, I reach through the bark and scratch its skin, which is rough and gnarled. It then flies away, howling and screaming."

"Wow! What's a screaming howler, Querciabella?", Gogzy asked.

"It's a servant, a worker for Ignis the Dark Elemental. I will tell you more of him later.

Screaming howlers fly, always in dark places or at night, roaming endlessly around the dimensions, even the human dimension, searching for a home to hide in, but they are mean, spiteful and never accepted. They aim to torment anyone they get close to.

They may show themselves to humans, and you have the *'sight'* to see them, Gazgy and Gogzy. Be on your guard.

They prefer to fly in darkness, but should one come close to you, never engage with it. They have dark, staring eyes and sharp beaks.

Should you ever be chased by them, or if they howl and scream at you, reply only by saying quietly, my name... *Querciabella...*

They will bullet into the sky, screaming and howling as they go. My name alone will throw them into a mighty muddle.

But more of that later…"

Gogzy shuddered, not keen on meeting a screaming howler at any time.

"You asked about my green hair, Gagzy. So, I will tell you, my hair is always a deep green shade in summertime, like the leaves of my oak tree. But if you see me in springtime my hair will be the bright green of the spring oak leaf.

And if you see me in Autumn, you might be surprised to see my hair has turned to a hue of yellow and red."

"Holy hairdos!", exclaimed Gagzy, with another of her choice phrases.

"You don't even dye it, Querciabella?", Gogzy asked.

"Does it just happen?"

"It happens with the change of the seasons.

As the colour of the leaves on my oak tree change, Gogzy, so does the colour of my hair, from the bright green of Spring to the deep green of Summer, and the yellowy red of Autumn. My hair and I, we live as my tree lives."

"What colour is your hair in winter, Querciabella?", Gagzy asked.

"In winter I sleep, Gagzy, just as my tree sleeps. And just as my tree loses most of its leaves in winter, I lose most of my hair as I sleep."

"Holy hairlessness!", Gagzy yelled, again, still unable to contain herself, she almost spilled her tea.

"A head with no hair!", she said.

"It's in fashion now, anyway. Some girls shave their heads."

"When winter ends do you wake up with no hair, Querciabella?", Gogzy asked.

"I do, Gogzy. But just as the buds on my oak tree return as the cold winter ends, so my hair quickly returns with the bright green glow of springtime."

"Unbeblubabable!", exclaimed Gagzy with another of her weird words.

"Gagzy, will you stop making up daft words!", Gogzy rebuked her sister.

"Do you ever get scared, Querciabella, sleeping all winter by yourself?", She asked.

"I don't feel fear, Gogzy. I'm never alone. Cumhachd is always by my side.", she answered, holding up the living tree branch which she always carried.

Gogzy's eyes opened wide with astonishment as she stared at Cumhachd's circular head. Did she imagine what she saw? Was Cumhachd smiling?

"Wow! I wish I had a Cumhachd, Querciabella."

"I'm always a bit scared of what might be creeping around in the shadows. What would you say to Cumhachd if you needed her to help you with something, Querciabella?"

"That's an easy question to answer, Gogzy. I would say simply *'Cumhachd, cuidich'*, meaning Cumhachd, help."

As Querciabella uttered those two words, Cumhachd leapt from her place in Querciabella's hand and stood beside her in the form of a huge golden eagle, the symbol of majesty, courage, and strength.

Cumhachd was taller than Gagzy.

"I would like you to meet Cumhachd in her preferred form. She is a golden eagle, but not one of your earthly dimension, Gagzy and Gogzy. Cumhachd is of my world and has greater powers.

You may pat her gently on the golden feathers at the back of her head. Just stand behind her, one on either side, and stroke her feathers, softly."

"Will she let us do that, Querciabella?", Gogzy asked in a whisper.

"She's so big, the biggest bird I've ever seen up close… And those talons on her feet, they are so sharp."

"Cumhachd has immense power, Gogzy, but she is also very gentle with those she cares for. Stroke her golden feathers and touch the curve on one of those sharp talons. By doing so she will trust you and you will become her friends."

The sisters stepped forward, gingerly, gently caressing Cumachd's feathers and touching the curve on one of her talons. She raised her head, proudly, in appreciation, before returning to her place as a branch of the great oak tree, held in Querciabella's hand.

"If you stay for a while you may yet see some of Cumhachd's powers. How long will you stay, Gagzy and Gogzy?"

"Well, we need to be home for our dinner at 5.00. But it's still early."

Gagzy looked at her phone.

"Oh, it's gone flat. It must be because we're inside the tree. But we still have plenty of time. We know the island, and we were amazed to see that building sticking out of the ground like a big pencil, when you spoke to us. Does anyone live there? We saw someone small, with a big head and little wings down beside the river. We thought he, if it was a *'he'*… We thought he might be watching us. Then he vanished."

"It was Misnich.", said Querciabella.

"He's a Pixie. He sleeps in the castle turret, together with many of his friends.

He's curious and mischievous, but he would mean you no harm. He spies on human sightseers and watches what they're doing."

"We guessed we were being watched, Querciabella.", said Gagzy.

"Misnich is one of the watchers. He and his friends like to live among the ruins of the castle. They love the history hidden in its ancient walls, the ghosts and phantoms who linger, hidden in the realm of the mysterious."

Immediately, as Querciabella spoke those words, a thought jumped into Gogzy's head.

'The ghosts and phantoms who linger… They must be real… If Querciabella says so, they must be real, hidden in the realm of the mysterious!'

Querciabella carried on talking.

"Some of the *'big folk'* have been visiting Eilean, Gagzy and Gogzy, *'big folk'* who don't have the *'sight'* which you possess. We are suspicious of them. Misnich and some of the Gnomes have been watching what they do. If they have bad intentions, they tell me."

"Are there Gnomes here too?" Gagzy was curious to know more.

"Yes, forest Gnomes. You will meet some.

We don't see them often in this part of Eilean. They are forest dwellers and mostly they live and work in the Eilean woods. But they fear an elemental which lives in the darkest, densest part of the woods. They speak to me about their fears, and they may seek my advice.

They too are watchers and guardians of nature.

They report to me about *'big folk'* who may harm nature or any of its creatures."

"Did they tell you we were here, Querciabella, because we know we were seen. Do they think we would harm nature?", Gogzy asked.

"Misnich told me he saw you. And he also told me you would harm nothing and no one."

"Thank goodness.", Gogzy answered.

"What's your age, Querciabella?", Gagzy asked, changing the subject.

"You look about the same age as me. I'm eleven, and Gogzy's eight. I'm the oldest but Gogzy's the smartest, especially with the meanings of words. That's why she doesn't like me making up my own words."

Querciabella thought for a moment before answering.

"It's a difficult question for me to answer, Gagzy, because you and Gogzy might not believe my answer.", she said smiling.

"My years are measured by the years of my oak tree. So, the age of my oak tree is also my age."

The sisters widened their eyes in surprise.

"I see by your surprised faces that you know I can't be the same age as you, Gagzy. Because you sit inside my great Oak tree, and you know it's not a sapling."

"Yikes!", exclaimed Gogzy.

"So, tell us Querciabella. How old are you?"

"I'm eleven, as you are, Gagzy. But then… I'm not eleven."

The sisters gazed at Querciabella, baffled by her answer, till she continued speaking.

I am one hundred and eleven years, the age of my tree."

"Yikes!", exclaimed Gogzy again.

"Crazy calendars! Unbecountable!", exclaimed Gagzy, inventing yet another word.

"Will you stop that, Gagzy?", said Gogzy, rebuking her again.

"Sorry, Querciabella.", said Gogzy.

"Gagzy keeps doing that, but it's hard for us to believe that's your age when we see the way you look, with your shiny green hair, your beautiful eyes and face, and your amazing clothes."

"I understand, Gogzy. But you should remember, both of you, I'm an elemental being, the spirit of my oak tree, and I age as one with my tree. It's simple. I am the heart and soul of my tree. As my tree ages, so do I, and my tree is yet young for an Oak tree."

"How long might your tree live, Querciabella.?"

"My Oak tree might live for eight or nine hundred years, perhaps more."

At that moment, Gagzy didn't have time for another crazy word, as there were five knocks on one of the windows.

"Ah! Five knocks. That means it's Misnich and the Gnomes, just as we were speaking of them. Shailagh may be with them. If she is, you'll like her. She is the Pixie Queen's daughter and a Princess.

You can meet them, yourselves.

Misnich might tease a little. He likes to be playful. And I should tell you, the Pixie tongue is unusual, for they speak always in whispers. They are gentle whisperers, so you may not hear their words. However, they can see you and understand what **you** say, because you have the gift, the *'sight'*. They know you have the gift, given rarely to those of humankind.

For that reason, they will understand **your** words, while they do not understand the words of others among the *'big folk.'*

One more thing, when they are happy and delighted, they make squeaking sounds.

The Gnomes are good fun too. They like to blether, but not in whispers. They are short in size and proud of their race."

"What's blethering?" Gagzy asked.

"It's just a kind of rambling on a little as they speak, Gagzy, sometimes making sense, other times, not so much sense. You'll see what I mean, but they are a proud and happy people, and very friendly.

Sometimes they like to tease each other, but it's all in fun."

The sisters gaped and wondered what might be coming next.

Querciabella walked to one side and touched the wall, the inner trunk of the tree.

Eilean Pixies and Eilean Gnomes

The side of the wall glowed for a moment and two tiny figures walked through, followed by another three, bigger visitors.

The bigger ones were the forest Gnomes, stocky and thickset, no more than thirty-six inches tall.

The girls recognised one of the Pixies as the figure they had seen beside the river… He was the Pixie boy with the big head, Misnich.

He had a raggy appearance, wearing a black, weatherbeaten jacket, red trousers, torn and tattered, held up by a scrawny brown belt.

A red pointed hat sat on his big head which helped him look a little taller. He wore black boots, curled upwards at the tips, and he carried a grey shoulder bag which seemed to bulge unevenly, with stuff inside.

Gogzy noticed his eyebrows were squiggly, like a worm on the move.

His friend was Shailagh, the Princess, and she was dressed in tiny clothes… but beautifully dressed as a Princess might dress.

Her blond hair was held up in a bun style and gripped tightly in place by a glittering gold band. She was like a little doll, wearing gold braided leggings, and a sleeveless top, tied at the waist by a little band with knotwork borders.

Around her forehead was a golden tiara, also with a knotwork design at the centre.

Like Querciabella, she wore no shoes.

Her little figure approached with white wings flapping silently, and floating across the floor to meet them, the sisters marvelled at her tiny beauty.

Looking very different, the three male, Eilean Gnomes followed into the chamber.

They walked with a hint of swagger, a proud walk, with shoulders swaying from side to side and footsteps in harmony.

They were short with big heads, big ears and big noses.

Each had the rugged look of forest dwellers, with nubby skin, and wearing homemade jackets and tartan kilts.

Their jackets were shades of blackish brown cedar bark with a black buckled belt around the waist. They had beards of different lengths and different colours, one red, one black, and one long and white.

Their kilts were knee-length, one in red tartan, one in green, and one in blue, each colour showing their Gnomish clan.

Unlike most Gnomes, Eilean Gnomes never wore shoes or boots. Their big feet were shoeless, bare and hairy. And they were noticeable for having huge, hairy hands.

On their heads were conical hats made from the smooth grey bark of the young elm tree. Each carried a shoulder-bag, one with builder's tools jutting out, another had small trowels and spades. The last carried weapons and tools in his bag, such as picks, hammers, and crossbows.

Eilean Forest Gnomes carried weapons for defence, not only of their homes, but also their treasures, hidden in burrow shelters.

Gagzy didn't know what to expect from the new visitors. Would they whisper or talk?

Gogzy stared in wonder, waiting for something to happen.

But what happened took both by surprise.

The three Gnomes squatted on the floor, close to the sisters and the fire, their legs crossed.

They stayed silent.

Misnich dropped his shoulder bag onto the floor and jumped up to Gagzy's shoulder, where he fluttered his wings at the back of her head, and tugged at her ponytail, squeaking. Was he laughing?

Gagzy felt her hair being pulled with the tug. It was just as Querciabella said… Fae folk could touch them as well as see and hear them.

"Heh!", she yelled.

"What's he doing, Querciabella? What's he doing?"

"He's tugging at your ponytail, Gagzy. They're excited. They've never seen a human inside my oak tree."

While he tugged at Gagzy's ponytail, Misnich whispered to Shailagh, telling her to join in the fun, so, she quickly jumped onto Gogzy's shoulder, but not to pull her ponytail. Her hair was hanging loose.

She combed her long red hair with a tiny comb, while whispering a reply to Misnich.

"What are they saying, Querciabella?", Gagzy asked, bewildered.

Querciabella translated their whispers.

"Misnich said, *'let's have some fun, Shailagh.'*

And Shailagh replied *'you should have asked first, Misnich.'*

So, just say *'hello'*, Gagzy.", Querciabella told her.

"They will understand."

"Hi, you guys.", she said.

"I hope you're having fun tugging at my ponytail, Misnich."

Misnich squeaked excitedly, before whispering some more.

"What's he saying now, Querciabella?", Gagzy asked.

"He said:

'She knows my name, Shailagh. She knows my name; she knows my name!'

He's excited and he repeats himself when excited, Gagzy."

Then Gogzy said:

"Hello, pixies. It's great to meet you. And thanks for combing my hair, Shailagh."

Shailagh answered, and Querciabella translated her whispered words.

"Shailagh says she is shining the strands of your hair with the magic of her comb. And I see your hair is sparkling, Gogzy, just like the shoes you are wearing."

Gogzy looked down at her luminous trainers, and with the side of her eye she saw her hair sparkle like twinkling star dust.

"Wow!", she answered, delighted.

After this introduction the Pixies jumped onto the table where they sat before the fireplace.

Querciabella introduced the three Gnomes.

"And so, Gagzy and Gogzy, I will introduce you to my other guests, the forest Gnomes sitting by the fire. They are loyal friends of Eilean, and they know well the threats we face. They know of dangers still to come.

"Aye, us ken well the dangers."

They had deep voices, dry and hoarse, and even though they were Eilean Gnomes, they spoke with a hint of a Scottish twang.

Querciabella carried on speaking.

"Forest Gnomes are a shy, retiring, peaceful race, as are the Pixies of Eilean, but neither will stand by and do nothing while Eilean is threatened."

"Aye, us ken them dangers. Us dinnae stand by."

They muttered in the same gravelly voices.

"Gnomes like to look their best to impress the lady Gnomes, as you will hear them say.

And each Gnome thinks of himself not just as *'himself'*, but as the whole of his clan. The members of each clan are strongly bonded. As are each of the three clans.

In any battle against Eilean, all three clans stand together.

I will introduce each one.

First, on the left is McNubby, who leads a clan of gardeners and diggers. Will you say hello, McNubby.

McNubby's hair and beard were long and white. He wore a green tartan kilt, and he stood to attention, big hairy hands gripping tightly his carrier bag filled with gardening tools.

"Hello, please misses. Us is McNubby, leader of clan McNubby us is, and proud is us to meet you. Us is earth workers… Aye, us is, just like papa, grandpapa, great grandpapa, and every McNubby who came before us. Everyone an earth worker and a digger. Proud of us history, misses… Us McNubbys… Us have the lumpiest skin of the forest Gnomes… Us do have the nubby skin to please us girlfriends. Them girlfriends, they love us nubby skin.

And us love us plants, misses… Us plants and us animals. Us love them."

He spoke with throaty, croaky, crackling tones.

"It's great to meet you, McNubby. I'm Gagzy… And plants and animals are my favourite subjects."

"And I'm Gogzy." Gogzy introduced herself.

"It's great to meet you, McNubby. Me and Gagzy, we've met a Gnome before. He's our friend, Lappy, and he lives in a beech tree. He's not as tall as you, and he plays with animals in our back garden."

Querciabella introduced the second of the forest Gnomes.

"Sitting beside McNubby is McKnobbly. Will you say hello, McKnobbly?"

McKnobbly stood to attention, wearing a blue tartan kilt. His beard was thick and red, and big hands gripped his carrier bag with builders' tools sticking out of the open top.

"Tis a proud pleasure to meet you, misses. Us is McKnobbly, leader of clan McKnobbly.

McNubby has the nubby skin but us clan McKnobbly… Us has the knobbly hands… Us has big hands… Us is builders and us knobbly hands come from them hammer bumps, and rocks fallin' on us fingers… Us is proud of us hairy, knobbly, big hands… Us is… And us girlfriends… They love us big, hairy hands and us big, hairy feet… And us is a peaceful people, but us won't stand by if that Dark Elemental gets awoken from its sleep by the *'big folk'*. Us is fearful of that Dark Elemental, but us won't stand by if it leaves its lair."

Gagzy gawked awkwardly at McKnobbly's huge hairy feet, wondering if she should complement him!

She decided not to.

"We love meeting you, McKnobbly.", she said.

"We don't know much about the doings of the *'big folk'* or a Dark Elemental who's asleep.

But we want to help Querciabella if we can."

"Yes, we do.", said Gogzy, even more confused than Gagzy as she stared with wide eyes at McKnobbly's big, hairy feet.

"We always want to help. And it's great to meet you McKnobbly.", she answered, wondering what the Dark Elemental might be.

Querciabella gave an explanation.

"I will tell you Gagzy and Gogzy, and all the Gnomes and Pixies, I will tell you more of a threat from the Dark Elemental when we know what that threat is.

There have been sightings, and recently there has been a sighting, by Whitewave, which was not threatening.

We think the Dark Elemental may be watching, just as we are watching, and waiting to see what the *'big folk'* may do next.

"Now I will introduce McKnuckly. Will you say hello to our human friends, McKnuckly."

McKnuckly stood to attention leaving his bag of weapons and tools on the floor. He had a long black beard and wore a red tartan kilt. He was tallest of the four Gnomes, about thirty-six inches tall, nearly one metre in height.

"Us is Clan McKnuckly, misses… 'Tis us has the biggest hands. Us girlfriends love big hands… McKnobbly's hands is big, but 'tis us, Clan McKnuckly, fighters and farriers us is… 'Tis us with the biggest hands… Us hands is biggest…"

McKnobbly frowned and cast an envious glance at McKnuckly's massive hands.

"It is us with the knuckliest knuckles…", McKnuckly carried on. Us is a peaceful people, misses, but if them *'big folk'* bring the fight to us forest Gnomes, us will be ready. Aye, us will."

Mcknuckly spoke in a voice, deep, strong, and croaky.

He clenched the fists of those huge hands and did a double fist punch into the air.

"It's great to meet you, McKnuckly. I don't think we've ever seen such huge hands. We're impressed, aren't we Gogzy."

"We're very impressed, McKnuckly.", said Gogzy.

"Such amazing big, hairy hands. But wouldn't you like to wear shoes or boots, Mcknuckly." Gogzy asked, unusually boldly.

She was taken aback when all three spoke together to answer her question.

"Och, no, no, no, no! Eilean Gnomes don't wear shoes or boots. Us girlfriends wouldn't speak to us again with them things on us feet!"

Gogzy didn't reply but stared back wide-eyed and speechless.

With the introductions over, the Gnomes sat again on the floor while the Pixies moved closer to Querciabella and began whispering in her ears.

Misnich first, then Shailagh, spoke in low whispers. This went on for about ten minutes, till, to the surprise of the girls, Querciabella spoke to the Pixies, also in a very low whisper, so low it was almost silent.

There was no squeaking.

"It must be a serious talk." Gogzy whispered to Gagzy.

Soon, Querciabella turned to the sisters.

"Misnich and Shailagh must go now. They tell me there are things going on near the castle ruins which they need to see. Some of the *'big folk'* have returned and are nearby, measuring things and taking samples."

"Us will leave with the Pixies.", said the Gnomes in unison.

"The woods wait, and the forest, it does fret. The Eilean trees do need us, need us they do.", said McNubby.

Misnich jumped and gave Gagzy's ponytail a friendly tug, before offering both girls a tiny handshake.

Shailagh offered an even tinier handshake, squeaking as she did so.

The Gnomes, in turn, bowed their heads to the sisters and followed the Pixies.

A moment later they passed through the space in the wall and were gone.

"Whoah!", Gagzy breathed a sigh, either of pleasure or relief.

Gogzy wanted to ask a question.

"Is it a secret… What you were saying to the Pixies, Querciabella?", Gogzy asked.

"It is a secret, but not to either of you, Gagzy and Gogzy. I always speak with Pixies in whispers, because it is their tongue, it is their way of speaking.

May I tell you why I met you with Whitewave and Anemone? May I tell you of our worries and how you might be able help us?"

The sisters stared at each other, not sure what to say.

Gagzy waited for Gogzy, who seemed nervous as she often did at moments like this, so she spoke for both.

"The people who are outside, those *'big folk'*…

They must have arrived after we did, but they may be the ones we saw on the boat, Gogzy.", Gagzy spoke to her sister who nodded.

"When we last came to the island, Querciabella, we knew we were being watched. But we didn't know who was doing the watching. Now we do. But we still don't know why.

So, I suppose we should listen if you're about to tell us why. Ok, Gogzy?", Gagzy wanted Gogzy to agree.

"Ok, Gagzy."

Querciabella lowered her voice almost to a whisper, but they heard every word.

"We face challenges, Gagzy and Gogzy, big challenges which may threaten our peaceful lives here in Eilean.

Firstly, the challenges will come from the *'big folk'*, people of your own race."

With all the talk about *'big folk'*, Gogzy had been wondering if she should ask a question about them.

Querciabella had just given them the answer… The 'big folk' were people of their own race…

But she asked the question anyway.

"So, are me and Gagzy part of the *'big folk'*, Querciabella?

"You are, Gogzy. But you are different. You are different because you have the *'sight'*. You have the gift to see beyond your own dimension. It is that gift which allows you to see and speak to me, and it is that same gift which means you may be able to help us here in Eilean."

The sisters listened to every whispered word as Querciabella continued.

'Big folk' have been watched by Whitewave, the spirit of the river."

"Just before we came up to the castle ruins, Whitewave spoke to us, Querciabella.", Gagzy told her.

"She said she foresaw beyond the present time, into the future, and that troubled times were to come."

"Yes, Gagzy, and Whitewave has watched *'big folk'* beside the river. What she saw has alarmed her as it alarmed me when she told me they prodded sticks into the water and made written notes about what they were doing."

She saw something else, something we know as the Dark Elemental.

This may be our biggest challenge. You heard the Gnomes speak of him. The dark Elemental is Ignis.

As an elemental spirit, he assumes different shapes.

As a Force of Nature, he is Fire.

He is a flaming, Brobdingnagian monster, an entity which rarely leaves his lair in the woodlands. We fear the recent arrival of the *'big folk'* has disturbed Ignis. He is one to avoid.

If you, Gagzy and Gogzy, decide to help us, I will show you an ancient hieroglyph which will allow you to step into the Tree of Life where you will be safe.

Inside the Tree of Life, you have protection from all dark dangers."

Gogzy's eyes widened, and her shoulders stiffened tightly around her neck, at this talk of an ancient hieroglyph and a flaming, Brobdingnagian monster.

And, unusually, she was stumped about the meaning of a word!

<<<<<<<< *'Brobdingnagian!'* >>>>>>>>>

It echoed in her mind. What might it mean?

She wanted to ask Querciabella that question.

Instead, she asked squeakily…

"What does it look like, Querciabella, this monster?"

"He is Ignis, Gogzy. He is a Force of Nature, as am I, Whitewave and Anemone.

In spirit, Ignis can be as dark as the blackest night, but in his outer form he is burning, blazing fire with flames of many colours. And in that outer form he has many shapes, just as a flaming fire has many shapes.

He rarely leaves his lair, but he has been seen by McKnuckle in the shape of a giant, black and yellow-spotted salamander, bigger than a dragon and longer than the longest snake, slithering through woods.

When McKnuckle saw him, he was breathing and snorting balls of fire from flaring nostrils.

If roused to anger, he makes screaming sounds.

Earth alone will not douse the flames of that monster.

Ignis has been seen by Misnich rising skywards like the Phoenix, spreading the plumage of his wingspan in flames of gold and scarlet.

But wind alone will not extinguish the flames of those wings.

And McNubby saw him, prowling, stealthily through the Eilean Forest, a lion with a fiery mane burning in red and white flames, surrounding his face and neck.

Water alone will not douse the flames engulfing that roaring lion.

McNubby took fright and ran like the wind to hide here, in my home, the Tree of Life.

Yes, Ignis is a Brobdingnagian monster, and he is at his most dangerous, when disturbed from a long sleep.

But if he is not disturbed, he remains calm.

Those who disturb him… They do so at their peril.

He will erupt in fiery fury.

But should that happen, it is my hope, we will overcome him and force him back to his lair."

The sisters stood back, wide-eyed, gaping with open mouths, at Querciabella's descriptions of Ignis.

Gogzy was panicky.

"But… But… But…", she stammered as she tried to ask a question.

"But why is he so bad, Querciabella?", she finally asked.

"Why is he so mean?"

"Once, in ancient times, he was one of us… Like me, Whitewave, and Anemone, he was a Force of Nature. We were four Forces of Nature, equal in our powers.

I told you at our first meeting, Gogzy, how we three are feminine Forces of Nature.

Ignis is a masculine Force of Nature, and there came a time when he demanded the old ways must change. We could no longer be equal in our powers.

The masculine Force of Nature must be the greatest power. The feminine powers of Earth, Wind and Water were not equal to the power of Fire.

And perhaps that is why we could not remain friends.

Ignis demanded that he should be King, like the lion is King of the jungle. He was the strongest so he must be Boss within our group…

One of us must be leader, he insisted.

We did not agree, and we refused. For myself, Anemone, and Whitewave, there was but one way forward.

We must remain as each being equal to the other. No single one should be Boss.

Ignis refused, and we were divided.

He was angry and he became angrier.

So, he began to pick on us, to bully us, one at a time, he bullied us. And through his bullying Whitewave learned that water alone could not douse his flames. Anemone learned that the strongest storm, by itself could not snuff out his fire, and I learned that earth alone could not crush his burning rage."

"Did he push you and shout at you when he bullied you, Querciabella?", Gogzy asked in her nervous voice.

"No… Not pushing and shouting. Ignis bullied with fiery power. He sent burning volcanic lava onto land and into seas. He filled fresh air with the black smoke of wildfires and forest fires, and he sent poisonous volcanic gases into the air as high as the clouds.

And so, the bullying continued until Anemone, Whitewave and I, we saw that by acting alone we would never match the intensity of his flames. But we learned, slowly, that by acting together, three were stronger than one, and, together, we were more powerful than Ignis, the Dark Elemental.

And so it was that we remained divided.

We became enemies, and still, we are enemies."

"Oh no! I'm afraid of Ignis!" Gogzy exclaimed in a panic.

"Please be calm, Gogzy. I don't tell you these things to scare you. But it's right for you to know what might come, should you decide to help us at this time, when we face threats from both Ignis and the *'big folk'*.

Whitewave foresees the Dark Elemental will leave his lair in the woods. And she thinks he will return unless the big folk drive him into a fury. She has yet to foresee that happening. We remain uncertain.

He may only want to know what the *'big folk'* are doing, just as we want to know what they are doing, and how they might affect our lives in Eilean.

Perhaps Ignis won't appear again. Much will depend on what the *'big folk'* are doing.

They are a different concern. They are your own race, Gagzy and Gogzy. I know this. So, I'll understand if you can't help us.

But I promise you this. While we worry the *'big folk'* may be a threat to us, we have no wish to harm them. And we won't harm them. We have our own ways of resisting intruders who would disturb our peaceful way of living. But we need your help. Because you have the *'sight'*. And this gift of yours may be the help we need to defend ourselves."

Querciabella stopped speaking, and Gagzy asked the question Gogzy had asked Whitewave.

"What did you mean, Querciabella when you said you came to reveal to us a mystery, and you told us:

'Change may beget change in another dimension'."

Querciabella paused, deep in thought, considering how she might answer Gagzy's question.

"This I will tell you, both of you…

In your dimension, where my Tree of Life lives, the leaves on my branches rustle in a breeze, and those branches bend and shake in a storm.

The wind causes these events to happen.

But when dimensions meet but never touch changes may happen in a different way. Change may beget change without any cause at all.

That is the mystery, and you will come to see the meaning of this mystery soon.

But first I must know more of the intentions of the *'big folk'*.

It is why we need your help, Gagzy and Gogzy."

"We want to help, Querciabella."

Gogzy stayed silent. She was deep in thought.

Querciabella carried on.

"Thank you, Gagzy. We think the *'big folk'* may be planning changes on the island which will be harmful to me and Whitewave, as well as Fae folk like the Pixies, and the Gnomes."

"Oh no!", exclaimed Gogzy.

Her thoughts were racing and drifting. She was thinking about the changes that might be coming.

"Why do they have to be like that, Gagzy? Why do they have to come here, and cause trouble among the people who live here?

Why do they want to do things that will upset the Fae people?"

"We only know what the newspaper told us, Gogzy. They want to build things.

We could ask mum and dad why they need to come here, but if we do, we can't say anything about Querciabella, the Gnomes and Pixies, or Whitewave, Anemone, and that Dark Elemental.

Mum and dad wouldn't understand, because they don't have the *'sight'* like we do."

"Gagzy is right, Gogzy.", said Querciabella.

"You're separated by your special gifts."

"Oh no! What can we do?", Gogzy, cupped her cheeks in her hands, as she often did when she wasn't sure about things.

"Do you know nothing of what the *'big folk'* are planning, Querciabella?" Gagzy asked.

"Almost nothing, Gagzy. But the watchers tell me they have been measuring things. They have been sticking things into my oak tree, causing me to shudder, and dropping things into the river, disturbing Whitewave's peace, and Pixies say they searched the remains of the castle and its leaning turret. Misnich whispered they were poking around the turret where he sleeps. He fears the *'big folk'* may plan to take it away.

Many Pixies sleep there. We must know more to be sure what might come next. Fae people watch them, but they can't ask questions or understand their words. And I can't talk to them as I talk to you who have the *'sight'*.

My hope is, Gagzy and Gogzy, that you might visit the castle ruins again and watch what they do, maybe ask some questions of them, and perhaps obtain some answers for us, so we might make our own plans.

I fear for my Tree of Life.

Just a moment ago, as I whispered to the Pixies, they told me that *'big folk'* have paced around it, as though counting their steps. And wrapped something around the trunk. Why? They don't know. And they pierced the bark of my tree twice with that sharp instrument, causing me pain, Gagzy and Gogzy."

Gagzy sighed a sigh of dismay, daunted by the thought of what might be about to happen.

"And the Dark Elemental, Querciabella. What if we see a lion on fire? Can it bite us?".

Gogzy plucked up courage to ask the question but feared the answer. Her voice was squeaky, not in a fun way like the Pixies, but nervous.

"As an elemental spirit, it can't bite you, Gogzy, because our two dimensions are separate. It can't become part of your dimension. But it may **appear** to be part of it. You may see and hear Ignis, as you see and hear me, but he cannot touch you. Our two dimensions are together in one place, but they never meet.

I will show you. Come closer to me and shake my hand, like you shook hands with Shailagh and Misnich."

Querciabella held out her hand and Gogzy walked towards her.

She reached out and grasped her hand. But she grasped only thin air.

"You see, Gogzy. As I told you when we first met, you may see and speak with me, but you cannot touch me. I am here with you only through your gift of the *'sight'*. I'm alive as you are alive. But we are in different worlds. Two worlds which never touch each other. So, the Dark Elemental cannot bite you. He's in the same place as I, Whitewave, and Anemone. He's an elemental spirit."

"But Misnich was pulling my hair!", exclaimed Gagzy.

"Pixies and Gnomes are not elemental spirits, Gagzy. They are Fae. And the Fae can meet and even touch those of your world who have the gift of the *'sight'*, as you have that gift. They can also be seen by animals. Often, they become friends with animals. And you may hear of others in your world who have met people of the Fae races.

The Dark Elemental cannot touch you. But take care… He may seek to scare you. Remember this advice I give you.

Remember too he is a Force of Nature, as am I, as are Whitewave and Anemone. And as a Force of Nature in your world he brings Fire. Should you see him stay well clear of his fire, as you would of any fire.

But know too that he cannot enter the Tree of Life. And if you decide to support us, you will be shown the secret hieroglyph, which will allow you to enter my home where it cannot follow.

I can say no more, Gagzy and Gogzy. I will await your decision."

Gagzy answered.

"Ok, Querciabella. Thanks for telling us these secrets. It's best we know the truth. I think we should go home now, Gogzy, and think about everything we've seen today, and everything you've told us, Querciabella. We'll come back tomorrow to tell you what we should do. Is that ok with you, Gogzy?"

"Ok, Gagzy."

The sisters said goodbye to Querciabella and headed for the boat trip home.

They saw two men and a woman pacing around the ruins as they left. The woman was carrying a clipboard and writing things on it. Gagzy spotted her immediately. It was the lady with the glossy, red lipstick.

Gogzy gawked, staring at her lips which were thick with lots of red lipstick… Way too much red lipstick!

She saw the sisters staring at her and scowled back at them.

The men carried tool bags and were also writing things onto clipboards. Gagzy saw one wore a big suit with stripes. He looked like a boss. The other wore blue dungarees and big brown boots. He was doing some digging and putting samples into a bag.

The sisters didn't approach them.

But they saw Misnich and Shailagh, watching what was going on, even fluttering around the shoulders of the lady with the glossy, red lipstick. They were easily seen by Gagzy and Gogzy but were invisible to the *'big folk'* as they went about their business.

"Those people look like some of the group we saw on the boat, Gogzy."

"Yes.", Gogzy agreed.

The girls carried on down the hill, where they saw another man and a woman on the riverbank, dipping things into the river and taking water samples. The man was older with a grey beard and wore waders for stepping into the river.

He had a dog with him, which Gagzy knew to be a Rottweiler.

The woman was young, fair-skinned with short blond hair. She had the longest earrings Gogzy had ever seen.

The girls passed them. Gagzy was tempted to speak.

"That big dog's a Rottweiler, Gogzy." she whispered.

"Don't say anything yet, Gagzy.", Gogzy whispered in her sister's ear.

But the Rottweiler had other ideas.

He was big, with black skin, and tanned parts on his face and legs. He ran towards them, jumping and wanting to play.

"Don't worry.", the man called.

"He's friendly. He just wants to play."

"Ok, thanks.", Gagzy called back.

"What's his name?"

"He's Gugzy.", the man called back.

"He's a big softy. And a great guard dog."

"Wow! He's one of us!", Gagzy answered, as Gugzy licked her hands and face, and she gave him a big hug.

"Welcome to the Gagzy, Gogzy, and Gugzy club.", she told him.

"We're just visiting." She called to Gugzy's owner.

"But we might be back tomorrow.

Bye, Gugzy, we must go for the boat now, maybe we'll see you tomorrow."

Gugzy barked and wagged his tail.

They walked on, in time for the boat home.

"I didn't mean to say anything, Gogzy. It was just when Gugzy ran to us it gave me a chance to introduce ourselves.

Now that Gugzy knows us it might make it easier to talk to them next time we see them."

"Ok. Do you think we should talk to mum when we get home, Gagzy. You know… About getting her advice, like Whitewave told us."

"I don't think so, not yet. I think we need to find out more about the trouble that's coming, before we ask for mum's advice."

"Ok, Gagzy."

Plans of the Big Folk

After a long, deep sleep, Gagzy and Gogzy headed straight for the treehouse, taking their breakfasts with them.

They climbed the rope ladder to Gagzy's tree bedroom where mum had left new jackets out for them.

"Brill!", exclaimed Gagzy.

"Our new jackets have arrived!"

Gogzy was excited. She looked at her reflection in Gagzy's mirror, fixed onto one of the tree's branches.

"Just what we need to cheer us up, Gagzy. Let's try them on. Mine's this green one.", she said, studying the mirror image.

"I love it, Gagzy. And yours too. I love the looping knotwork design around the rim of your hood, and down the sides of your zip. It's just like the looping design on the carpet of Querciabella's Tree of Life."

"Yup, me too, Gogzy, let's wear them today. Let's wear them on the trip back to the island."

Gogzy's thoughts quickly returned to the events of yesterday.

"But I can't stop thinking about yesterday… And the *'big folk'*, Gagzy. That's us! We're the *'big folk'*. Even Querciabella said it. So, we can't pretend we're not.

We're still kids but we're human people, and that makes us part of the harm the grown-ups will do to Querciabella, Whitewave, and the Fae people if they change the island. I don't want to be part of that. We must help stop them doing the stuff they're going to do.

I just don't know how we'll do it, Gagzy.

That lady with the glossy, red lipstick, she isn't someone who would listen to us. I think she's jealous of our special gifts. And that bossy looking man with the stripy suit, we can't tell him what to do. He looks like he's in charge of it all.

We saw them with their tools and clipboards, and they were doing things beside the river. What were they up to, Gagzy? What will happen to Whitewave if they start doing things to the river? And they've been sticking things into Querciabella's oak tree. It's terrible!"

"Maybe the first thing to do, Gogzy, is to find out more about their plans. We could ask what they're up to without being cheeky. Thanks to Gugzy, we've met some of them. That might make it easy to talk to them, when we go back.

So, should we rush back and hope we can make them stop? Or should we stay at home because we're too young to **tell** them to stop what they're doing?

They might just laugh at us and tell us to go away.

Let's see if the newspaper says any more about their plans. We didn't read all of it, only the bits about the skeleton with no feet."

Gagzy picked up the newspaper and turned the pages away from the headline front page.

"Yes, here it is, in big black print on page seven.

Plans for Moreau Island

I'll read it out, Gogzy.

This is what it says:

Moreau Island has been sold to new owners. They own everything on the island except Tower Hall.

They own the woodlands, the ruins of Moreau castle, and Moreau River.

The new owners are allowed to remove the ruins of the castle and change the site by making a golf course.

"But Gagzy, if they take away the ruins, they'll be taking away Misnich's home… And it's not just Misnich, but the other Pixies who live there with him. Surely, they could leave the turret where it is.

And they own the woodlands. That's what you just said. But that's where the Gnomes live! What might they do with the woodlands?"

"I've asked mum about planning, Gogzy. She said they would need permission for their plans.

Maybe something can be done about that. But I'll just read the rest of the newspaper. It might say someone can complain about their plans.

Oh, dear, the next line in the newspaper isn't good. It says this:

One tree must be chopped down, and it is the oak tree near the castle ruins."

"Oh no, Gagzy! Oh no! Oh no! Not the oak tree, That's Querciabella's home! They can't chop it down, Gagzy. Tell me they can't chop it down."

But, as she read more, Gagzy couldn't find anything to say the tree was safe.

"Help! This isn't good, Gogzy. It's not at all good. I better read the lot before we get too upset.

The new owners are allowed to change the river. It must run in a straight line towards the sea. The zigzagging flow of the water is a problem for their plans."

"Yikes, Gagzy! It just gets worse and worse! It's not only Querciabella, the Pixies, and the Gnomes which are threatened, but Whitewave too. They can't change the course of the river without changing her. And what harm will it do to the creatures who live there, like the otter we saw. What will become of them? Oh no! What might happen to Querciabella?", she yelped, cupping her face in her hands.

"Are you sure you want me to say the words, Gogzy?"

"Say the words, Gagzy. Tell me.", she sobbed, knowing what was coming.

"Well… You heard what Querciabella told us, Gogzy. She lives as her tree lives; she changes as her tree changes. If the oak tree is killed…" A tear dropped from Gagzy's eye.

"Oh, no! Help! Don't say it, Gagzy! You shouldn't have said it."

Gogzy's thoughts were thrown into turmoil…

The sisters sat in silence, each gaping and waiting for the other to speak.

At length, they spoke the same words at the same moment.

"We must do all we can to help save the ruins, the oak tree and the river."

There was more silence till Gogzy decided they would need a plan.

"We won't let it happen. We must make our own plans. Where should we start Gagzy?"

"Well, after you went to bed last night, I asked mum what planning permission was, because she knows about that stuff through her job. She said people can't just go ahead and build things… They must get permission, so, she said she'll check on that and tell me more later.

And I told her how the new owners were sticking things into the oak tree and measuring it and all that. So, she said there's something called a Tree Preservation Order… With some trees, you can't just chop them down.

Mum says there are rules about oak trees. They get looked after. She said she would find out what she can about the one on Moreau Island."

"That's a good start, Gagzy. So, let's wait and see what mum finds out. And we need to go back and start talking to those people… Those *'big folk'*… We can act like we're nosy kids, asking what's going on, and once we find things out, we can tell Querciabella what we know."

"Yes, but should we tell her what they're planning to do with the oak tree, Gogzy? She would know what that means for her."

"Let's not say anything about that until we find out more from mum. Maybe they won't be allowed to chop it down. Maybe the newspaper has made a mistake. But listen, if we tell Querciabella what those owners tell us, we need to know their names. We don't know their names, so let's make up names for them."

"Ok, Gogzy. We saw three men and two ladies, didn't we, so what should we call them?"

"Ok, how about:

1. The lady with the glossy, red lipstick.
2. The lady with the blond hair and long earrings.
3. The man with the stripy suit.
4. The man with the blue dungarees, and…
5. The man with the Rottweiler.

"Not bad, Gogzy, now we know exactly who we're talking about, even though we don't know their names. So, let's pack our bags, mum's left us a packed lunch. We can get the next crossing at 12.00."

"But shouldn't we talk to mum, Gagzy, now we know more about the trouble that's coming to the river and to Querciabella. Maybe we should ask for mum's advice now."

"I think it's best if we have another visit to the island before we do that, Gogzy. We'll see how quickly their plans are moving if we go back today. We can talk to mum tomorrow."

"Ok, Gagzy.

Big Changes

The sisters headed for the passenger boat, proudly wearing their new jackets, and they were surprised at what they saw.

"Look, Gogzy... Boats one, two and three! What's going on? And they're all different sizes! Ours is the smallest one.

There's about twenty people queuing up to board the middle one, and that third one, the biggest one, it's gigantic! And what's all that stuff it's carrying?"

There were already five people and a dog on the smallest boat which never carried more than eight passengers at any time.

"Oops! Who's that on our boat?", exclaimed Gagzy.

"Do you see who I see sitting on our boat, Gogzy?"

"I do, Gagzy. It's the new owners, and Guzzy, the dog. And the lady with the glossy, red lipstick, she's there too with a mean face. I don't think she ever smiles."

"Ignore her, Gogzy. We can talk to the others.

This could give us a great chance to chat to them, but the journey takes only seven minutes. So, get your thinking cap on Gogzy. Ask the right questions and we might find out what they're going to do on the island, and when it's happening.

But what are those other boats beside ours? We should ask them about that too if we get the chance."

"I'm not sure about the big boat, Gagzy, but it looks like it's getting ready to leave. And it's full of stuff... Loads of stuff. Maybe it's a cargo ship, with all those big machines it's carrying."

"I'm worried Gogzy. It's pulling away and I think it's heading for Moreau Island, same as we are. And look, the second boat with all the people, it's following the big one."

The sisters boarded the passenger boat to the delight of Gugzy who sniffed and spotted them at once.

"Hi, Gugzy.", Gagzy gave him a hug as he rested his big paws on her shoulders and licked her cheeks.

"Do you remember us from yesterday, Gugzy?"

The lady with the glossy, red lipstick looked snootily at the girls but said nothing.

The man with the Rottweiler spoke first:

"I think you've made a friend. He's a big softy but he doesn't take to everyone. You must be special.

So, you're on another trip to the island, but you don't live there. I know that, because no one lives there."

"Yes, we just like to visit on our summer holidays from school.

But what's that big boat with all the heavy stuff on it? Why is it going to the island? And the smaller one with all the people?"

The woman with the glossy, red lipstick looked uppishly at Gagzy, as if to say, *'what business is it of yours?'*

But she stayed silent.

"Oh, that's a cargo ship carrying our gear. We'll be working on the island, making changes. And the boat following it, that's the one taking our workers.

We're just starting, but when you visit next summer, you'll find an exciting new place. There will be a lovely new hotel, chalets and caravans, and new attractions for kids, like an outdoor swimming pool. The ruins of the old castle will be gone, but we're keeping the dungeons. Not many visitors know about the dungeons, because they're buried under rubble now. But we'll make the dungeons into an exciting place for kids who like a good scare!", he said laughing.

"We'll have that skeleton running around with no feet. And we'll have its feet running around with no skeleton! So, do you like a good scare?", he asked laughing.

"No, not really.", Gogzy answered. She didn't think it funny to talk about the skeleton like that.

"But what about the river? We like the river. It's lovely, with the trees and plants along its banks, and all the birds nesting there. We saw an otter yesterday."

"Oh yes." The man in the stripy suit replied.

"The river will still be there, but with a few changes. I'm afraid the otters will have to go. They might be a risk to kids like you. They can get angry. Did you know that? Otters can get angry if they feel cornered. So, we'll need to put them somewhere else."

"That's not right, Gogzy.", Gagzy whispered in her sister's ear.

"They can't just move them from their home."

"But the river is their home. They live there.", she was annoyed as she spoke to the man with the stripy suit, but he wasn't interested, ignoring her comments.

"And there's beavers too.", he told them.

"Those pesky beavers are worse than the otters, with their dam building. Proper pests they are. They'll have to go too."

Gagzy was unhappy about making the otters and beavers live somewhere else. She wanted to say:

'How would you feel if someone came to your house and told you to leave because you might scare the kids next door?'

But she said no more, thinking she was too young to argue.

"But what about that skeleton with no feet?", Gogzy squeaked, wanting some serious information about it.

"Who found that?"

"It was me.", said the man in the blue dungarees.

"I was digging when I saw a finger sticking out of the soil, and there it was when I dug it all up. A footless fellow it was."

"Aye but being a footless skeleton didn't stop it trying to make a run for it, did it?", the man in the stripy suit chipped in with a grin on his face.

Gogzy stared at him with one of her wide-eyed stares.

"I grabbed it before it could reach the moat and sprint down the hill… Caught him on the run, I did. It won't bolt again if I'm around."

"He's pullin' your leg." said the man with the Rottweiller.

Gogzy remained unamused. They were determined to make a joke of it.

"What other changes will there be?", she asked.

The lady with the glossy, red lipstick answered. She was annoyed by all the questions.

"Don't be nosy.", she snapped.

"You ask too many questions."

"It's ok.", said the man with the Rottweiler.

"They're just curious. Did you tell me your name yesterday? What's your name?", he asked Gogzy.

"I'm Gogzy, and this is my sister, Gagzy."

"Well, Gogzy and Gagzy. As I say, we're developers and we'll be making a lot of changes on Moreau Island. We're changing the landscape to make a golf course. We'll clear away the castle ruins and there's a big oak tree near the ruins. We'll get rid of that. It's smack bang in the middle of the spot where the hotel will be. So, it's bye-bye oak tree."

The man in the stripy suit interrupted.

"We can sell the oak. It will fetch a good price."

The sisters gasped, silently, staring at each other, wanting to scream out their anger and dismay. Hearing the developers say these things, sitting right beside them, was much worse than reading about it in a newspaper.

The man with the Rottweiler carried on.

"We'll build a hotel and some chalets, and, to fit all this in we need to change the shape of the river. It's too wide for the plans we have, and it's too *'ziggy zaggy'*, if you know what I mean. It's a big job, and will take nearly a year, that's why you saw our heavy gear on the cargo boat. We'll need diggers and dumper trucks to do the work. And tents for our workers to live in. There isn't a hotel for them to use. Let's face it, ours will be first!", he said proudly.

"But by next summer it will be an exciting place for you kids to visit."

A thought jumped into Gagzy's head.

'I bet we'll have to pay!'

"Will we have to pay when we come next summer?", she asked.

This time it was the man in the stripy suit who spoke again.

"Darn right you will. I ain't doin' this for charity. I'll be lookin' for a good return on my investment… Darn right you'll have to pay."

"What's an investment?", Gagzy asked.

"It's money! That's what it is. It's when you put money into a business to get more money out of it. Money makes the world go round. It sure does."

"Our teacher… She says it's the sun that makes the world go round and round.", said Gogzy.

"And she'll be right about that, lass.", said the man in the stripy suit, with a grin on his face.

"But money's hotter than the sun, it sure is."

"Is it not greedy to want too much money?", Gagzy asked.

"You can't get enough of that stuff, lass. You'll find that out soon enough.", said the man in the stripy suit.

"Our great grandpa says if we get greedy for too much money, we'll turn into selfish misers with no friends.", said Gogzy.

The man in the stripy suit didn't have an answer to Gogzy.

He just made a silly, surprised face!

But the girls were sad, feeling they had learned all they hoped **not** to learn. These developers didn't care about the oak tree or the river on Moreau Island. It was money they cared about.

Gogzy decided to ask another question.

"Where will the chalets be?"

The lady with the glossy, red lipstick scowled, looking daggers at Gogzy for being even more nosy.

The lady with the blond hair and long earrings had said nothing until now. She was wearing pink, tight-fitting leggings, a white summer jacket, and black high-heeled shoes. *'How will she walk on the rough ground?',* the thought crossed Gagzy's mind.

The lady answered Gogzy's question in a posh but friendly voice.

"I'm the architect for the project.", she told her.

"The chalets will be along the hillside, and the building work will start when we fix the zig-zagging flow of the river. The river must flow in a straight line down to the sea."

The boat reached the jetty, and she rose from her seat to leave, as did the man in the blue dungarees. The man in the stripy suit followed them.

The lady with the glossy, red lipstick was last of the group to rise from her seat. She scowled at the sisters before turning to them.

"Remember what I told you before.", she whispered.

"If you're planning any magic trickery, I want to know about it. If there are ghosts, goblins, elves, trolls, or grunting, growly Gnomes, I want to know about them. Do you hear me? Do you hear me?" She screeched in a screeching whisper!

"I want to know how you know about them." She snarled and turned away to follow the others in her group.

"She really doesn't like us, Gagzy."

"She's pretty horrible, Gogzy."

"Have a fun day, Gogzy and Gagzy.", said the man with the Rottweiler as he alighted from the boat onto the jetty, with Gugzy in tow, wagging his tail excitedly.

As they left the boat, the sisters stared at the scene.

The massive lorry with gigantic thick wheels was first to disembark onto the slipway. It was perfect for driving over rough ground.

Then a huge crane on the cargo ship hoisted trucks, diggers, skips, and other big machines onto the back of the lorry. Those machines would change Moreau Island, and the river which flowed down to the sea.

"Look at all the people carrying tool bags and back packs, Gogzy. They'll be workers. But where will they sleep?

There's no hotel on the island. There's so much to tell Querciabella, and it just all seems to be bad for her and the Fae people."

Gogzy was deep in thought, only half hearing her sister's words.

"Oh no, Gagzy! I don't know how we'll tell Querciabella about all we've learned.", she sighed.

"I know. It's not good news. It's seriously **bad** news! But it's best we say nothing yet about what will happen to the oak tree."

"It's so terrible, Gagzy!"

Naughty Invisibles

The sisters decided to stick around for a while, watching the offloading of a big container box with the word…

'PORTALOOS' written on the sides.

And there were stacks of smaller boxes, crates and hampers, all packed with goods going onto the back of the huge lorry.

"Portaloo… That's a toilet, isn't it, Gogzy?

"Yes, they're toilets that can be moved from one place to another.

There aren't any toilets on the island, so they'll need them, Gagzy."

Hundreds of packs of bottled water and tins of food arrived, food and water for the workers. There were no shops on the island.

Another big container was lowered onto the lorry.

Written on its side in large print was the word… **TENTS.**

"So, that's the tents where the workers will be sleeping, Gogzy. Gosh! There's so much stuff coming off that boat.

It will bring big changes to Moreau Island, and it makes me think about what Whitewave and Querciabella said to us…

It makes me wonder about the mystery…

It was a mystery about how changes in one dimension may bring about changes in another dimension, wasn't it, Gogzy?"

"You're right, Gagzy! And **Yikes! Yikes!**

I understand! I think I know what the mystery means.
All the stuff that's about to happen on Moreau Island… It will make things happen on Eilean too…
That's the mystery…
That things happening in one dimension can make things happen in another!
It's a mystery because it can't be explained.
How could something happening in our world of Moreau Island make something happen in Eilean?
This is like when we met Penny, the ghost of Tower Hall.
We changed things in Penny's ghostly world by changing things in Tower Hall.
That's what rescued her from her lonely fate as a ghost.
Now we can do the same for Querciabella and Whitewave.
But first, we **must** stop the developers from changing Moreau Island.
That's the mystery, Gagzy! The changes here will beget changes on Eilean, and…
Why were they telling **us** this?
It's because they **knew** they needed **our** help. They knew they could talk to us because of our psychic gifts.
That's what's going on, Gagzy? Am I right?"

"I think you've just solved the mystery, Gogzy. And I get it too.", said Gagzy, suddenly enlightened by Gogzy's words.

"The dimensions never touch, but they are linked in a mysterious way. And I don't want to say it, Gogzy, but what happens in Eilean… It will be bad… It will be very bad if we don't stop the developers from changing everything here on Moreau Island. We know what will happen to Querciabella, don't we. We know it for certain.

It's why she came to say those words… '*I come to reveal to you a mystery*'."

The sisters had seen enough.

They knew Moreau Island would be changed overnight into a tent town full of workers.

And they knew the peace of the secret island would be broken. The flow of the Eilean River would be disturbed just as the flow of Moreau River would be changed.

And worst of all… It seemed the removal of the Tree of Life would mean the **end** of Querciabella as an elemental spirit of Eilean?

They walked fast, saying little till they arrived at the site of the ruins and stood beside the oak tree, hearing the flow of the river as it rolled along the hillside, below the rickety bridge, and onwards to the sea.

Gagzy hugged the tree, as far as her arms could stretch.

"I am so sorry Tree of Life.", she said sobbing.

"What can we do to save you?"

The branches of the tree whispered a rustling reply, but not in words the sisters understood.

She turned away, her eyes scanning the grassland, the space which would become the golf course.

"Gogzy, look ahead of you, across the grassland and the tree groves. They've started already with the golf course. They must have been here yesterday.

The holes are there in the ground. Someone is walking to each hole, placing a flag in it, and giving it a number.

And look… There's a truck filling a space with sand. That's a bunker for the golf course."

"Yes, but look over there, Gagzy… That man with the flags, someone is following him, and do you see, the one following him… He's tiny.

He's walking and fluttering alongside the man who doesn't even know he's there."

"I see it, Gogzy. But something's happening… Just as the man drops the flag into the hole, the wee guy pulls it out again and throws it to one side. And now… What's he doing now?

Hah! He's taking a pouch from his bag and pouring stuff into the hole! He's filling in the hole!

Gogzy, I think the little guy is a Pixie! Do you see? That pointed hat he's wearing; it's a Pixie hat. The man with the flags can't see him, but we can.

That's brill… When that man carrying the flags looks back to check on his work, he's in for a shock. The flags will all be lying on the ground. The holes will be filled in! And he'll be scratching his head. He'll be baffled!

I think the Pixies are starting to fight back already! Come on, the Pixies!", Gagzy yelled.

The man looked to see who was calling. The sisters giggled and turned away.

"What happens now, Gagzy?" Gogzy's tone was upbeat and excited.

Gagzy didn't have time to answer, because, from amid the gorse bushes, Misnich emerged, followed by seven other Pixies, each dressed as he was, in rags, but in various colours, all wearing curly-toed black boots, and pointed hats. The girls knew which was Misnich, because he wore the same colour of clothes as yesterday.

They muttered and chattered in whispers. Misnich led the way, pointing a tiny finger towards the trail of flags thrown aside. The others rolled on the grass squeaking in Pixie laughter.

Misnich ran forward and tapped the bark of the oak tree five times, the number of knocks which told Querciabella who was outside.

Gagzy and Gogzy stared at the tree bark.

After the five knocks, its colour softened and lightened. Misnich signalled to the sisters to follow, and they did so, walking through the trunk as though it wasn't there, followed by the other Pixies, whispering excitedly.

The mood of the Pixies had raised the girls' spirits, but the tough job of telling Querciabella the news was still to come.

She appeared, radiating the same glow as when first they saw her.

"Gagzy and Gogzy. I'm so happy you've come back. And I love the design of your jackets. It's beautiful. The knotwork pattern is very like the one on my carpet, the Tree of Life."

"Thanks, Querciabella.", they answered together.

"We knew they would match your carpet."

"I asked Misnich and his friends to look out for you. Sit by the table."

They sat in the plump armchair, while Misnich and the Pixies vanished up a rope ladder onto a higher floor.

"I've been told by Misnich and others there is much activity outside and all around the Tree of Life. Have you had time to think? Have you decided?"

"You, go first, Gagzy.", Gogzy prompted her sister.

"Yes. We have decided.", Gagzy answered.

"We decided yesterday that we wanted to help.

We read more in a newspaper about what would be happening, and we made up our minds we wanted to help. Then today, coming across on the boat, we learned a lot more. We met the people on the boat, the ones in charge of changing things here in the castle ruins, and in the river. And we think now we know what you meant when you told us you came to reveal a mystery to us."

"I see.", Querciabella answered.

"Thank you for giving support to our cause, Gagzy and Gogzy. But I detect you are sad. I fear your news is bad news."

"It's terrible, Querciabella!", Gogzy blurted. Knowing the outlook was sad, her feelings took over.

"They're going to build houses and a hotel, right here where your tree is, so lots of people can come and stay for a while. And they're going to make a stupid golf course, so people can hit a wee white ball with a stick, until it falls into a hole in the ground. And they plan to change the river, so it doesn't zig-zag. And they're bringing trucks and diggers and toilets and tools… And tents for people to live in. It won't be the same, Querciabella.

The castle ruins will be gone… and… and… and…"

Gogzy forgot they decided to say nothing about the fate of the oak tree. Her feelings and tears made her forget.

But she couldn't bring herself to say the words she dreaded. She fell silent, sobbing quietly.

Gagzy hugged her, a tear in her own eye, knowing the words Gogzy couldn't say.

"Be at peace, Gogzy. Be calm.", Querciabella told her.

"I think I know the news your kind heart can't reveal. So, I will say the words for you…

The Tree of Life blocks the path of the *'big folk'*. It stands in the way of their progress. And so, it must be removed."

"They're going to chop it down, Querciabella.", Gogzy sobbed.

"But, be at peace, Gogzy, for the task, which is to be done, is not yet done… And that which is not yet done, may yet remain undone. And so, the defence begins."

Querciabella rose from her seat and looking upwards, above the hanging rope ladder, to where Misnich and his friends had gone, she called his name.

"Misnich."

She turned to Gagzy and Gogzy.

"I'll speak with Misnich and his friends, Gagzy and Gogzy.

I'll give them instructions, and they will start a peaceful resistance, a defence of our secret island.

And now you know the meaning of the mystery, you know that Eilean will suffer. So, we must defend Eilean.

'Big folk' will not be harmed.

Pixies are masters of mischief making, and though they may be small, they are fickle little foes who win their battles without hurting anyone."

Misnich descended the rope ladder followed by seven others.

Rapid whispering followed with Querciabella doing most of the whispered talking.

When they finished, Misnich gave Gagzy's ponytail a friendly tug then darted to a corner of the room.

It was then the sisters noticed something they hadn't seen when they entered the tree.

Someone was busy in the corner, and Misnich and his friends went to speak to him.

"Who's that wee guy, Querciabella?", Gagzy asked.

There was a tiny visitor, sweeping and scrubbing the floor.

"He looks like a hobgoblin.", said Gogzy.

"We used to see them in our house and garden."

Querciabella was about to tell them who the little guy was, when Misnich ran, then fluttered, across the room and whispered to her. She nodded a reply, and he left with his friends.

The little guy joined them, each walking in single file, and they disappeared through the trunk of the tree.

"To answer your question Gagzy, the one who looks like a hobgoblin is a Broonie.", said Querciabella.

"He cleans for me, tidies up, washes some of my pots and pans, and I feed him in return. He and other Broonies have also noticed the *'big folk'*.

They don't want them here in Eilean. They want them to leave.

A Broonie can be scary, and very angry. In anger he may become a boggart and reveal himself to humans… Something which isn't allowed, but boggarts don't care what's allowed or not allowed.

Misnich knows this and he will tell the Broonies how they can help.

Pixies and Broonies… They're very good at making a nuisance of themselves, especially towards humans if they don't want them around.

You saw them leave, Gagzy and Gogzy. You saw Misnich and seven of his friends. He has many more friends. And you saw the Broonie. Together they will cause problems for the *'big folk'*.

Others will come forward in defence of Eilean, Gagzy and Gogzy. All is not yet lost."

"Will the Broonie be angry with me and Gagzy?", Gogzy asked.

"Will he turn into a boggart to scare us?"

"The Broonies know you're here, Gogzy. They won't be angry at you, because they know I'm your friend."

"We've seen so much today, Querciabella.", said Gagzy.

"There is so much going on outside, we just don't know how it can be stopped.

We can tell you what we've seen and what the *'big folk'* are saying, but to them, we're just kids. If we complained, they wouldn't take us seriously. If we told them to stop what they're doing, they would just laugh at us and tell us to go home."

"I understand, Gagzy, but you're already helping us, and you will help us further. This assault on Eilean won't be stopped in an instant, but step outside the Tree of Life, both of you.

Walk through the trunk where the bark shines and see the scene around you. Then come back the same way and tell me what you saw. This will give you encouragement."

The sisters entered the glowing part of the trunk and walked through.

The sight which met their eyes took their breath away. They gasped.

Across the grassland which would become the golf course, tents of every description were pitched.

"How can they be there so quickly, Gagzy?"

"I'm gobsmacked same as you, Gogzy. Maybe they're those kinds of tents which just spring up by themselves when you press a button."

"But what about that huge one in the middle. It's half the size of a football field."

Gogzy pointed towards a Marquee tent which was as big as a big building, and its sides were being held in place by ropes pinned to the ground and pegs which men hammered into the grassland.

"The men are still working on that one, Gogzy. It looks like it's nearly finished."

The tents had many shapes. There were bell tents, which looked like a big bell. Others were pod tents with more than one room, while others were dome shaped see-through bubble tents with seats inside.

Most of the rest looked like pop-up tents of different sizes, the kind which sprung into shape in an instant.

"Wow, I wish the tents weren't here, but it's amazing how quickly this tent town has appeared. It's like someone waved a magic wand, Gogzy!"

"Aaagheeee!"

"What was that, Gagzy? Someone just screamed."

"Look, there, Gogzy... The pink pod tent, just left of the bell tent. Look who's running out of it. She's lost one of her shoes. It's the lady with the blond hair and the big earrings."

"Aaagheeee! Get it away from me. Get me out of here."

She screamed again and ran to the hillside, with one high-heeled shoe off and one high-heeled shoe on, she was trying to escape something. The man in the stripy suit stopped her.

"What's happened?", he asked.

"What are you running from?"

"Get out of my way. I'm leaving. Find someone else to plan your hotel. I'm leaving and I won't be back."

She bolted, downhill, tumbling clumsily as she ran on her single high-heeled shoe, in the direction of the jetty where the boat was moored.

"What just happened, Gagzy?"

"Look, Gogzy, standing beside the tent she just ran from. Do you see it?"

"I see it, Gagzy. That goblin... Is it a goblin?

The lady with the blond hair and the big earrings must have seen it. It's horrible! And she's been scared to bits. She said she's leaving, and she won't be back."

It stood at the tent entrance, about 18 inches high, half a metre tall, with long skinny arms and three-fingered hands, hanging below its knees, almost down to its huge feet. Its toes were twitching, some curling upwards, some downwards, and looking like hooks.

Its head was about the same size as its body, with a dirty, green face, sharp-pointed ears, one tiny pig-like eye on the middle of its forehead, and three nostrils on a nose which twitched from side to side. Its mouth was wide open, showing black curly teeth, some curling upwards, some downwards, with sharp points at the ends.

To make things worse, its black tongue drooped down out of its mouth, twitching hungrily, like it was searching for something, or someone, to eat!

It was as horrible, and as scary as anything the sisters had ever seen, scarier than a fiendish goblin.

It wore a dirty black jacket and short, raggy trousers.

Gugzy the dog raced forward, barking angrily at it. His owner, the man with the Rottweiler, rushed forward.

"What's wrong with you, Gugzy. What are you barking at?"

Gugzy's barking turned to a fearsome growl, but the creature showed no fear. With its one eye, it stared back at Gugzy, like it wanted to stare him out. Some black saliva dripped down its tongue onto the ground.

Gugzy didn't back off.

It raised its three-fingered hands towards Gugzy as though it was about to grab him.

"The man with the Rottweiler can't see it, Gogzy. It's only us and Gugzy who see it. Gugzy should run!"

But Gugzy didn't run, and the thing didn't pounce. It just stared out of its one eye.

Was it afraid of Gugzy's fearsome growl?

"What is it, Gagzy? What are we seeing? What are we looking at?"

"Maybe I'm wrong, Gogzy, but I think we're looking at an angry Broonie switched to a boggart. And I think it must have shown itself to the lady with the blond hair and the big earrings. She must have jumped in terror, losing one of her shoes.

Look at it! It's not moving. It's just staring back at Gugzy. Maybe it has never seen a dog before."

"Gugzy is so brave! But what should we do?"

"Come on, Gogzy, let's run down there and take a closer look. Querciabella says the Broonies know we're her friends. And a boggart is just an angry Broonie. So, it won't harm us."

"No, I'm not going near it. That lady with the big earrings was running for her life. She was terrified."

Gagzy grabbed her sister's hand.

"Come on, we'll be fine."

"Gagzy, the Broonies know we're Querciabella's friends, but that boggart doesn't!"

Gogzy yelled as her feet started running with the pull of Gagzy's hand.

They rushed forward across the grassland, past the huge Marquee tent and stopped at the entrance to the pink pod tent.

The man with the Rottweiler was there with Gugzy, who was calm and quiet. The boggart had vanished.

It looked like Gugzy had won the staring battle.

Seeing Gagzy and Gogzy, he wagged his tail and cuddled into them, sniffing and licking.

"It's Gagzy and Gogzy!", said the man with the Rottweiler.

"You're just in time to keep Gugzy happy. He was about to go bonkers, barking crazily at nothing at all. I don't know what spooked him."

"Did you see anything?", Gogzy asked.

"Only our architect running away without her shoe."

He picked up the missing shoe from inside the tent.

"She ran like the clappers, tumbling down the hill.", he told them.

"We heard her screaming. She said she was leaving and wouldn't be coming back.", Gagzy replied.

"We'll just have to find someone else to do the drawings for the hotel. Now, Gagzy and Gogzy, I'm having a busy day, and I don't have time to keep Gugzy amused. Would you do me a big favour and look after him for a while?"

"We would love to.", they answered together.

"Fantastic.", he fixed Gugzy's leash to his collar and handed it to Gagzy.

"He pulls a bit sometimes, Gagzy, but you're a big strong girl.

When you're leaving to go home you can return Gugzy to the blue tent next to this pink one. That's where I'll be… Bye."

The sisters strolled off with Gugzy in tow, casually taking in the busy scene around them, as more people arrived.

After the shock of seeing the boggart, they saw at once this wasn't a normal buzzing scene of people being busy. Something didn't fit.

Some of the people didn't fit!

"Gagzy, what on earth is going on? Do you see them?"

"I see them, Gogzy. And it explains why Gugzy is tugging so much. He sees them too! And he wants to play and sniff them. He can see them, but can he sniff them?"

What they saw were Pixies, many Pixies, and a few Broonies, not boggarts, all mingling with *'big folk'* who were unaware of the little people playing and having fun.

"Look, Gagzy. Do you see her? It's Shailagh! Her hair is still tied up in a bun, but she's wearing shorts now. And look there are other girl pixies with her. Do you see them, Gagzy? They're all wearing shorts!"

"I see them, Gogzy. What's the word for a girl Pixie?"

"Gosh, I don't know. How about Pixette?"

One Pixette, wearing a yellow pointed cap, jumped on Gugzy's back, jumped off again and tugged at his tail, before fluttering behind the girls, tugging at their hair.

The princess Shailagh and others followed, joining in the tugging.

Shailagh fluttered around their heads, waving both tiny hands before following her friends who flew over to the Marquee to join others in the job of pulling out tent pegs. *'Big folk'* had hammered the pegs into the ground to tighten the ropes supporting the tent. Without those pegs that giant tent would fall. The Pixies and Pixettes were mischief making!

The pegs were hammered around four sides of the tent, and the sisters gazed at *'big folk'* workers who stood back, hands held aloft, dismayed at the sight of the mighty tent collapsing to the ground.

"What's going on?", someone yelled.

"I told you to hammer those pegs in deep and get a tight stretch on those guy ropes."

It was the man in the stripy suit whose eyes didn't see the gang of Pixies laughing and wrestling each other on the grassland.

The Pixies had removed all the pegs, and the huge tent fell to the ground in a bundle.

They celebrated by wrestling. It was one of their favourite ways of having fun.

The sisters giggled, and Gugzy barked, sensing the good mood. He tugged at Gagzy's grip on the leash till she let him go. He wanted to be part of the fun.

He jumped onto the scrum of wrestlers, sniffing and barking excitedly, his big paws padding the Pixies as he joined in with the wrestling game.

He turned to Gagzy with a confused, questioning look, rotating his head as dogs sometimes do.

If he could speak, he would probably ask *'What's going on? Who am I playing with?'*

He had never romped and frolicked with so many tiny people.

"He really loves to play with them.", said Gogzy.

"Yes, but Gogzy, we've seen plenty. The Pixies are fighting back.

They've toppled that huge tent.

If the Pixies can do this, that Marquee tent will **never** stay standing.

Let's go back and tell Querciabella what we've seen."

"What about Gugzy, Gagzy? Will Querciabella let him come in?"

"Yes, she loves animals."

Back at the Tree of Life, the white light of the tree bark was still aglow, and the girls walked through with Gugzy by their side.

What happened next was surprising.

"This is Gugzy.", said Gagzy.

But Gugzy didn't bound forward with his usual excitement. He padded softly towards Querciabella, pining, like he was seeing someone he had been missing all his life.

"My dear friend.", was all she said.

She didn't touch Gugzy, who squatted, almost like he was asleep, completely at peace.

"And so, Gagzy and Gogzy, tell me, what have you seen outside the Tree of Life?", Querciabella asked.

"We've seen loads, Querciabella!", They announced excitedly together.

"I'll talk first.", said Gagzy.

"The tent town has sprung up like magic. One minute it was all crates and boxes, big and small, the next minute, the tents are all standing, except the biggest one, the Marquee."

"Guess what, Querciabella.", Gogzy jumped in excitedly, interrupting Gagzy.

"The Pixies are everywhere, having fun and causing big problems. Some Broonies are there too. That big Marquee tent just collapsed. The Pixies pulled out all the pegs holding the ropes, and the tent collapsed."

"And that's not all, Querciabella.", Gagzy spoke again.

"We saw the blond lady with the big earrings. She's the architect, the one in charge of the plans to build the hotel, and she was running away, leaving one of her shoes behind and tumbling down the hill. She was scared, screaming and yelling that she wouldn't be coming back!"

"And guess why she was scared, Querciabella.", Gogzy jumped in again, even more excitedly.

"She had seen a boggart. She was terrified out of her wits. And we saw it too, from a distance. Then Gagzy wanted to get closer to it, and we ran across the grass because Gugzy was barking and barking and barking at that boggart. But when we got there the nasty boggart was gone."

"That's when we saw the Pixies pulling the tent pegs out of the ground and the Marquee tent collapsing, Querciabella.", said Gagzy.

"And it made the Pixies laugh and wrestle, seeing how they succeeded in pulling down the Marquee tent."

"This is why I wanted you to see how things were moving forward.", Querciabella answered.

"What you tell me helps me decide what to do next. And it allows the invisible Pixies to set about their job of stopping the *'big folk'*… It's a step towards making them change their plans.

All is not yet lost. You are helping us greatly to save Eilean and our way of life.

Perhaps you should go home and rest now, as the task that lies ahead is greater still."

"Ok.", Gagzy answered.

"We'll take Gugzy back to his owner. We'll come back tomorrow."

As they walked towards the jetty where the boat was moored, the sisters chatted about what might be coming next.

"I suppose we must talk to mum, Gagzy. I think it would be best if we do that right away, as soon as we get back."

"I think you're right, Gogzy. I'm getting a feeling that those developers want to do things as quickly as they can. So, it's best we talk to mum as soon as possible and don't leave it till tomorrow."

"But how do we do it, Gagzy? Whitewave told us that trouble lies ahead for Eilean, and we are to ask mum's advice. But how will we do it without talking about Elemental beings, Pixies, Gnomes, Broonies and boggarts. How will we do it, Gagzy?"

"We just need to find the right words, Gogzy."

Advice from *'the'* Mum

Back home, the girls told mum as much as they could about what happened on Moreau Island, without talking about Elemental spirits or Fae people.

That was the price for their special gift of the *'sight'*.

They couldn't share that gift with anyone else, not even their own mum, because she just wouldn't understand.

To tell her about other dimensions would only make her worry that they were going back to their old ways of talking about hobgoblins, faeries and ogres.

They had learned a lasting lesson when they spoke too much to school friends about the Fae people. It only got them into trouble, **big** trouble.

So, they spoke to mum only about the developers' plans to change the course of the river by stopping its zigzagging flow to the sea.

They told her how the curve of the river was a problem. The shape of the river must change if chalets were to be built.

And those creatures living on the riverbank, like otters and beavers, they would need to be moved.

And they spoke to her about the tent town which had sprung up suddenly, like magic, so the builders would have somewhere to live for the next year.

Everything on the island had started to look and feel different.

And they told mum of their biggest fear, that the great Oak tree, the Tree of Life, was to be chopped down to make way for a hotel.

"What can we do mum?" Gagzy asked

"We hate what will happen to the island."

"It depends on the planning permission, Gabriella."

Mum rarely used the girls' nicknames.

"I spoke to your dad about it, and he says you're not the only ones who don't like what's happening on the island. There are others who will complain.

But if permission has been given to change the course of Moreau River, then it's unlikely that will be revoked."

"What's *'revoked'*?", Gagzy asked.

Gogzy jumped in to answer.

"It's just a fancy way of saying the planning permission won't be changed, Gagzy. They will still have permission to change the river.", she explained.

"Well, we'll just have to see about that, won't we, Gogzy."

Gagzy was thinking Whitewave and Anemone might have other ideas.

"Did you find out about the rules about oak trees, mum... About some trees being protected."

"I did, Gabriella. It's not good, but it's not completely bad.

The developers own the land, so they can remove the tree. But if they **weren't** allowed to chop it down, there would need to be a rule saying:

'***The oak tree is protected***'...

And it would be written in papers they received when they bought the island.

I've asked for a copy of those papers, but they may take a while to arrive."

"That's great, mum."

"So, keep your fingers crossed for the Oak tree until the papers arrive. But if it's not protected, all is not lost.

We could ask for a Tree Protection Order. That's a T.P.O. for short. I'll deal with that part.

And there are other things you can do to help."

"We want to help as much as we can, mum, so tell us what we can do. What can we do?", Gagzy asked, keen to press on.

"Well, you can draw more attention to what is happening to the oak tree... Let people know how you feel. Make some noise about it, girls. I know better than most how good you are at that, you especially, Gabriella.

You could put a post on the internet. Start a petition complaining about the changes on the island. Copy it to your friends and even to the newspaper which wrote about the plans and the gentleman with no feet."

"Mum!", Gagzy yelled.

"It wasn't a gentleman. It was a 700-year-old skeleton!"

"Of course. And remember… very important… Children have a **right** to protest, so long as it's a peaceful protest. You have as much right to protest as any adult.

So, start your own protest to save the Oak tree on Moreau Island, and the castle ruins. Use the social media to invite others to visit the island to see for themselves the magnificent Oak tree which is threatened. Don't give up on the Oak tree yet.

I'll ask your dad to have a police officer there on the day of your protest. The officer will uphold your right to protest. That's the law. Children have a right to protest if they think something is wrong."

"We're lucky to have dad as a police officer.", said Gagzy.

"This is pure brill mum!", exclaimed Gogzy excitedly.

"You give great advice! I can't wait to tell Querciabella."

"What a beautiful name, Gloria. I don't think I've met Querciabella. Is she a school friend?"

Gagzy puffed her cheeks at Gogzy's slip-up.

"Em…em…em…em." Gogzy was befuddled.

When she was forced into telling a fib, she just couldn't do it, especially to mum… Usually she stuttered and stammered till Gagzy came to her rescue, as she did now.

"She's a girl we met on the island mum. We'll probably see her again when we go back."

"That's nice.

So, you can start making plans. Perhaps Querciabella will join you. You can take my voice amplifier to make yourselves heard when you start your protest. You can use it to shout so loud I might be able to hear you over here on the mainland.

So, when will you start your protest?"

"What do you think, Gogzy. How about the day after tomorrow?", Gagzy asked.

"Yes, let it be the day after tomorrow, Gagzy. That gives us more time to prepare."

"So, I will start your online petition now.", said mum.

"You can ask people and friends to support it, and we'll print some copies for you to get signatures on the protest day.

She switched on her laptop and started typing:

"It should be something punchy for a heading.", said Mum.

Moreau Island. Save the Castle Ruins. Save the Oak Tree.

"How about that?"

"Brill!", they answered together.

"And the wording of the petition text?", she asked.

"I think we should mention our main worries, Gogzy, but keep it short."

"Ok." Gogzy agreed.

"So, you say first, Gagzy."

"But can I make a suggestion?", said mum.

"I suggest you start by using the words…

'Stop the changes to Moreau Island.',", said mum.

"Ok.", said Gagzy.

"Let's say that mum. Then, Well… I think we should say…

We oppose:

1. Building a hotel and golf course which will spoil the peace of the island.
2. Removing the ancient castle ruins.
3. Changing the flow of Moreau River to build chalets.
4. Removing otters and beavers which live on the riverbank.
5. Chopping down the Oak tree, the beautiful Tree of Life which lives amid the castle ruins.

Please show your support.

Sign blow…

How does that sound to you, Gogzy?"

"Really good, Gagzy. I second that."

"Well done girls. And I suggest you finish by saying… 'Please support our plea for a Tree Protection Order for the Oak tree and sign our online petition.

And you're doing the protest the day after tomorrow, so dad will arrange for a police officer to go with you on that day, and I'll have petition papers ready to hand out to people.

So, remind me to give you my portable voice amplifier. You should do the shouting Gagzy."

"Mum, you're a star.", said Gagzy.

"A twinkling star.", Gogzy agreed.

The Pain of Whitewave

They rose early next day, keen to get to the island before the developers rushed ahead with their plans.

Mum put some packed lunches into their bags.

"You look very pretty in your new jackets with the Celtic embroidery.", she told them.

"I'll have the paper petitions printed by tomorrow.

Say *'hello'* for me to your new friend, Querciabella. Did she like the embroidery on your jackets?"

"She has a whole carpet in her house, embroidered with the Tree of Life, mum.", Gogzy answered, before hastily covering her mouth, realising her mistake.

It was another slip-up.

"She told us about her house, mum.", said Gagzy, rescuing Gogzy from saying any more.

The boat was at the jetty, and a few minutes later they were heading along the cliffside towards the rippling flow of Moreau River and the castle ruins on the hilltop.

The scene had changed from yesterday. It had changed completely with the arrival of more trucks, parked along the riverbank.

But they weren't vans or lorries. They looked more like trucks used to transports farm animals.

Men carrying animal handling poles with nets on them were returning the poles into the back of a van. It seemed like they had finished using them.

As the sisters approached, sounds coming from inside the trucks grew louder.

They heard an anxious commotion of animals barking and yelping.

The sides of the trucks had air slats and the animals causing the commotion weren't sheep or cows from a farm. They were wild animals from the river.

In one truck they saw the howling, brown faces of beavers with beady eyes and orange front teeth. They made distress signals of hissing, growling, and grunting, while they battered their tails angrily against the sides of the truck.

In another they saw the wide eyes, long whiskers and short muzzles of otters, peeping between webbed feet pressed against the open slats.

Some made chirping sounds like scared birds, while others hissed, growled and barked … Captured and locked away from their natural home beside the river, they were scared and desperate to escape.

"What a racket, Gogzy. How can they do this to these animals? They belong in the water, not stuck inside a truck. This is just wrong! How can they do it?"

"I know, Gagzy. Look at this wee one."

Gogzy pointed to a smaller face yelping through one of the spaces on the side of the truck.

"It looks like a baby otter, Gogzy. It's maybe separated from its mum."

"What are you doing here?" A voice sounded behind them.

They turned to see the lady with the glossy, red lipstick together with the man in the stripy suit.

"We're just visiting again. It's our school holidays. We like to visit the river.", Gagzy answered, not ready to say too much about their plans for a protest.

"This is a site for development and investment. It's no place for you two. Now, be on your way."

The lady with the glossy, red lipstick was unfriendly as usual, just as before.

But Gagzy wasn't being pushed away that easily.

"You don't own those animals.", she told her, stiffly.

"And our dad's a policeman. He said we can still come here. He says someone has complained about your plans, and you might have to stop what you're doing. And you shouldn't be putting otters and beavers into those trucks. It's cruel. It's just mean and cruel."

"We have a licence.", said the man in the stripy suit.

"We have permission to move these animals. Now, on your way. You can play near the ruins if you like."

Gagzy and Gogzy moved away. They were just by themselves. They didn't want to argue with grown-ups. Tomorrow a police officer would be with them. They would have more confidence, and they would have their petition to hand out.

They walked further along the riverbank to be met by a sad sight, one which no other would have noticed.

What they saw would have been invisible to anyone else.

A trio of figures sat on a grassy verge of the riverbank.

The sisters recognised Querciabella at once. She was comforting Whitewave who was sobbing, seeming wretched and heartbroken.

The third was Anemone.

She sat facing Whitewave, with the outline of a hand on her shoulder.

They saw Anemone through the shining, billowing streaks of hair which screened her body.

She was almost shapeless.

"I think Whitewave is crying, Gogzy. She seems very upset." Gagzy spoke as they walked to meet the trio.

"Do you remember the nymphs of Erehwon, Gagzy. We met them in the Kingdom of the Fae. Anemone looks like one of them."

"She does. Let's see if we can talk to them."

They approached the group and Querciabella spoke first.

"Gagzy and Gogzy, we're pleased to see you, even at such a sad time.

Whitewave is deeply saddened. Her animal friends, the river otters, and nature's builders, the beavers, are being captured by the *'big folk'*. She hears their cries for help, but she can't interfere."

"It's worse still…", Whitewave sobbed.

"Those *'big folk'*… They'll take away my animals, my river dwellers, they'll take them to another place, away from their home.

And they are digging the land where the river curves. They will replace it soon, with dams which will change the flow of the river.

I am a Force of Nature, and as a Force of Nature I am present in your world. But as an elemental spirit I am in the dimension of Eilean, I am the river of Eilean.

Changing the river in the natural world also changes the Eilean River."

Whitewave's words confirmed what the sisters had learned about the mystery… The mystery they had come to reveal to them… That what happens in one dimension may beget changes in another.

Whitewave carried on speaking and sobbing.

"This will sadden my heart, and it will change my spirit to one of pain and sorrow, driving me deep into the depths of the sea, where I will weep streams of tears.

My friend, Anemone, will be angry that they hurt me.

She will blow a mighty storm, driving surging waves across the oceans onto the shores of the *'big folk'*.

They will run in fear of the power of her storm.

This will happen through the folly of the *'big folk'*, and the harm they do to nature."

Gogzy stared wide-eyed at the silhouette, which was Anemone, in awe at this description of her power.

"We have a plan, Whitewave.", Gagzy said, feeling Whitewave's pain.

"We have spoken to another.", said Gogzy.

Whitewave's sobbing slowed. Her mood lifted a little.

"Did you seek the advice of the mum?", she asked.

"We did.", the sisters answered together.

"We asked the mum for advice.", said Gagzy.

"Will you take that advice?"

"We will. We've made our preparations." said Gagzy.

"And we'll come back tomorrow, to carry out her plans. And we won't be alone. Others will support us."

"Your news is uplifting, Gagzy and Gogzy. This news will change my *'foresight'*.", said Whitewave, her sobbing fading.

"It is true.", Querciabella agreed.

Their conversation ended and the trio of elemental spirits vanished.

The sisters climbed the hill to witness changes from the day before.

Gagzy was surprised by changes on the site of the castle ruins.

"The bushes!" she exclaimed.

"Where have all the gorse bushes gone, Gogzy?

It looks like those developers are wasting no time. They're pressing on fast. Maybe they know there might be objections to their plans, and they want to get things done before they can be stopped."

Misnich's turret was still there, but most of the rubble was cleared.

The gorse bushes which had covered the hilltop were cleared, to make way for the building work still to be done. The Tree of Life stood alone.

A banner encircled it with the words:

KEEP OUT   LUMBERJACKS ONLY

    NO ENTRY

THIS TREE IS TO BE FELLED

At its base lay saws and cutting machines.

Each of two big machines had the words *'FELLER BUNCHER'* written on its side.

"Lumberjacks only. That's the people who chop down trees. And what's a *'Feller Buncher'*, Gogzy?", Gagzy asked.

Gogzy knew the meanings of most words.

"I don't know that one, Gagzy."

"I'll look it up on my phone, Gogzy."

Gagzy gulped as she read the meaning of the words.

"It says it's a motorised machine that can cut a tree's branches before chopping it down."

"Oh no!", Gogzy yelped.

"Those feller bunchers weren't here yesterday. They must be planning to do it soon, Gagzy. That must be why that banner is wrapped around the tree. It's so everything is ready for the chopping to start!"

"It won't be today, Gogzy. They're too busy with the animals in the trucks. But we best come back early tomorrow with our petitions, and mum's voice amplifier too, so we can stop them using the feller bunchers."

"Yes, Gagzy. But look over there at the turret, where the gorse was before. Look what's at the base of the turret. We can see it better now. It's the trap doors to the dungeons below."

"Let's take a closer look, Gogzy."

They crossed the clearing to the turret.

"They've been busy here too, Gogzy. The doors leading to whatever is down there are locked.

If we go down there, it won't be today. And if that skeleton with no feet is down there, he won't be able to get out. Thank goodness he won't be able to escape." Gagzy was making a silly joke.

"Don't make jokes, Gagzy.", said Gogzy, nippily.

"I won't be going down there at any time! I'm staying above ground. So, let's move away from this trap door."

"Ok, maybe we've seen enough, Gogzy. It's my guess they're rushing things. They told us it would be a year to finish all the building work.

But what have we seen today?

Look at how they're rushing ahead with the changes to the flow of the river and moving the otters and the beavers. They're worried! They're worried objectors might be coming to put a stop to that.

And why are they so desperate to chop down the Oak tree, using those nasty feller bunchers?

The lady with the big earrings ran away, so, there's no one to start the plans for the hotel.

They're rushing ahead with these things before they can be stopped. I'm guessing that's what's going on, Gogzy."

"You're right, good thinking, Gagzy. And if they're in a rush to spoil the river and kill the Tree of Life, then we should be rushing too. Let's get home and check with mum if everything is ready for tomorrow."

They walked down the hill, heading for the jetty where the boat would be waiting.

"Heh, look Gogzy, look what's going on down by the riverbank, where the trucks are with the otters and the beavers. Take a good look, because we're the only ones who can see them."

"I see them, Gagzy. That's Misnich wearing his red trousers and his red pointed hat. It's Misnich and some of his Pixie friends."

"Look what they're doing, Gogzy. Misnich is carrying a big set of keys. He must have pinched them from one of the workers. He's going round the six trucks. He's opening the shutters at the back of each truck. His friends are going inside and shooing the animals to jump free. Look, Gogzy, dozens of otters and beavers jumping into the river. They're free again!"

"Yippee!", Gogzy yelled.

"Oh! Oh! What's happening now, Gagzy? It's the lady with the glossy, red lipstick and the man with the stripy suit. They are not happy!"

"Who opened the shutters on the trucks?", she screamed at the workers who were running around with pole nets trying and failing to catch the escaping animals.

"My keys!", someone shouted.

"They're not in my pocket. Who took my keys?"

"There are keys lying here on the grass.", said another picking them up.

"Who opened the shutters?", yelled the man in the stripy suit.

"Who took those keys?"

"Look!", yelled the lady with the glossy, red lipstick, pointing towards the hillside, seeing Gagzy and Gogzy descending.

"It's them! Did you take those keys to set the animals free?", she shouted angrily.

"We've been playing on the hilltop, just like you told us to do. We have no keys.", Gagzy called back to her.

"If I see you back here again, it will be the dungeons for you two. There are ghouls down there… Ghouls who don't like girls… Do you hear me? Ghouls who don't like girls!

You'll make some new unfriendly friends when I send you down those dungeon stairs.", she yelled.

Gogzy looked scared, as she wondered why ghouls don't like girls.

"We'll be back tomorrow with a police officer.", Gagzy answered.

"Come on Gogzy, let's head off home."

As they moved away, they heard the man in the stripy suit call out orders to his workers:

"Forget the animals for now. We'll deal with them later. We can't waste any more time chasing them. We start work on the dams immediately. Fetch the steel, the timbers, and the plastics. Bring in the diggers and get the cement mixers ready. Use the new cement mixer truck. Be careful with it. It's an expensive bit of kit."

The sisters hurried off, jogging the rest of the way.

"Well done Misnich and his friends.", said Gogzy, still wondering why ghouls don't like girls.

"Yes, the beavers and the otters are back in the river, and that will make Whitewave happy.", said Gagzy.

"But they're starting work on the dams, Gagzy, and that **won't** please Whitewave."

"As usual, you're right, Gogzy. The dams are what they will use to make the river flow in a straight line. That's what will hurt Whitewave even more.

If only they knew the harm they will do."

They arrived at the jetty as the sky clouded over, and they heard a clap of thunder.

The weather changed as the boat returned to the mainland where they found a crowd of people gathering on the beach and looking towards Moreau Island.

And as they stepped ashore, the wind whipped up and they heard roaring, rumbling sounds, the kind a train makes when it's travelling fast on the tracks.

Was a storm coming?

"What a racket, Gogzy. What is it. And why are all these people on the beach?

"I don't know. They're pointing towards the island. And look there's mum and dad in the crowd."

They dashed over to meet them.

"Heh, what's all the noise, mum?", they yelled as they ran.

"Turn around, girls. Look towards the island. You're just back on time. We were worried.", dad shouted.

"Holy mushrooms! It's a giant spinning mushroom!", Gagzy yelled above the rumbling roar.

"Maybe it's a big umbrella, Gagzy." Gogzy yelled into her sister's ear.

"There's lightning too!", someone in the crowd shouted above the noise.

"It's not a giant mushroom, Gabriella. And it's not a big umbrella, Gloria. It's a tornado. I've never seen one in Scotland." Dad called out to make himself heard.

"The round part at the top is cloud. The funnel-shaped part below the cloud… That's what's spinning and making the noise you hear. The sound is coming over the sea, and that makes the noise louder."

"We were praying you were on the boat, girls.", said mum.

"Being close to a tornado is no place to be."

"Anything caught inside that spinning funnel is spun around, and it picks up nearly everything in its path.", said dad.

"Wow!", exclaimed Gogzy.

"What if there are people around, dad? There are people on the island right now. We saw them just before we left."

"They must run for their lives, Gloria. They mustn't get close to that spinning funnel, or they would be spinning around inside it along with broken glass, rocks, dirt, and objects of every kind, big and small. If they do get sucked in by that tornado, they might be lucky and get hurled into the sea. Hopefully they can swim."

"How long will it last, dad?"

"Not long, Gloria, maybe fifteen or twenty minutes. When it starts to lose energy, it peters out."

"Yikes! Look, it's moving. It's not just spinning in one place, it's moving around! It still has energy!" Gogzy yelled at the top of her voice.

"But look how it's moving, Gogzy." Gagzy shouted into her sister's ear above the din.

"Look at the shape of the movement. It's zigzagging, like the zigzagging shape of the river. What does that make you think, Gogzy?"

"I know what you're thinking, Gagzy.", Gogzy yelled back.

"You're thinking it's **following** the same zigzagging shape as the river, aren't you."

"Yes, this is more than a tornado, Gogzy. It's following the curves of the river. This is a tornado with a name.", she yelled into Gogzy's ear, knowing no one else could hear what she said.

"This tornado is Anemone… It's angry Anemone, showing how angry she is at what they're doing to Whitewave and to her river."

"Gosh, Gagzy. You are right. Anemone is spinning furious!"

The gathering of people on the beach stood in awe for another five minutes, maybe a little more, till the tornado slowed and faded.

"It's starting to disappear. The excitement is over.", said dad.

"I hope those people on the island managed to hide well away from that spinning funnel.", said mum.

"And with all the excitement we haven't had time to introduce you to Sophia."

"Yes," said dad.

"Here she is, right beside me, Constable Sophia.

And these two red-haired mischief makers are my daughters, Gabriella and Gloria.

Sophia will accompany you tomorrow morning on your protest march. We can only spare her for one day, but that should be enough to make it known you have the full backing of the police for your protest. And I'll give you a display notice saying that."

"We prefer our nicknames, constable Sophia. I'm Gagzy and this is Gogzy."

"Ok, I don't have a nickname, but, since it's only for one day, it's ok just to call me Sophia. I'll be here waiting to meet you both at 10 a.m. tomorrow.

I'll be wearing my police uniform, so people will know I enforce the law. Mum and dad have told me all about your online posts, your petition and how you want a Tree Protection Order. So, I'm well prepared for the visit. See you tomorrow morning."

Constable Sophia said goodbye, and mum, dad, and the girls carried on home.

"I think there will be a lot of interest tomorrow.", Mum said as they walked.

"There has been a big response to my post about the oak tree on the network."

"And what about the Tree Protection Order?", Gagzy asked.

"I've heard nothing yet, but I've mentioned the application in my post. And I've made some phone calls to people who know about these things. Someone may arrive on the island when you're handing out your petitions."

"That's great news, mum. We can't wait to get started.

I just wonder how much mess there might be after the tornado.", said Gogzy.

"Well, it's not our job to tidy it up, Gogzy.", said Gagzy.

"Those developers can do that."

The Protest

They arrived early for the first boat of the day to find Officer Sophia waiting. And she wasn't alone.

Three boats were moored at the jetty and a queue had formed.

"It seems the posts your mum put online have been successful, Gagzy and Gogzy. There has been a big demand for tickets, so, there are two extra boats to bring people to the island, and each boat can carry eight passengers.", Sophia told them.

"Brill!", exclaimed Gogzy.

"I love your jackets with the Celtic embroidery around the rims and the hoods. It's a lovely design."

"Thanks, we like them too."

"Now remember, you have every right to protest, Gagzy and Gogzy, so long as your protest is peaceful.", she told them as they made the short crossing on the boat.

"I see you're carrying a portable table, Gagzy, and you have fold-down seats, Gogzy."

"Yes, Officer Sophia. These are for us to sit with our petition papers so people can sign them."

"Very good, but just for today, call me Sophia."

"Ok, Sophia."

They alighted from the boat and walked to the hillside and the riverbanks.

"After the tornado, I expected a mighty mess.", said Gagzy.

"But everything is quite tidy. It looks like lots of stuff has been moved."

"Maybe the tornado moved them.", said Sophia.

"Isn't that what your dad said. It will suck up everything in its path."

Workers were gathered and they seemed to be squabbling and distracted like they didn't know what to do.

There was no sign of the developer bosses.

Along the riverside where the flowing river curved and zig-zagged, none of the big machines were there. They had been moved.

"Can we ask them what's going on, Sophia?"

"Let's do that, Gagzy."

"Hi.", Gagzy spoke to the group of workers.

"We're here to get signatures for our petition. Constable Sophia is with us. We wondered what's going on after the tornado."

A man stepped out of the group, and the sisters recognised him as the man with the blue dungarees, the one who dug up the skeleton with no feet.

"We can't carry on with the job of building dams to straighten the river.", he told them.

"All the materials, and the machines have been sucked up by that tornado. Even the cement mixer truck, it's a big heavy machine, it was gobbled up too, and everything dumped onto the beach.

It's like that tornado had a mind of its own! So, we won't be building the dams any time soon."

'Brill!', Gogzy chuckled silently to herself. But her excitement was cut short.

The man in the blue dungarees hadn't finished speaking.

"We've been told we've to start work on the felling of the oak tree. We're just waiting for the gaffer to arrive."

"When will you be doing it?", Gagzy asked

"Today, I guess. Some of the guys are preparing things right now at the top of the hill."

"That's where we're going with our petition. So, we'll just go up there now." Gagzy told him.

"This isn't good news is it, girls?", Sophia asked as they walked up the hill.

"It's terrible news!", exclaimed Gogzy, frantically.

"They've just cancelled one nasty piece of work on the river and replaced it with another on the hilltop. Oh no! They're going to kill the Tree of Life! And they're doing it today, when our petition hasn't even started!"

"Don't despair, Gogzy.", Sophia told her.

"Look behind you, walking along the cliff edge. More people are arriving. And more will follow. Your protest is just beginning. You can set up your table and chairs at the top of the hill."

But more bad news awaited them at the top. Enclosing the Oak tree, a barricade was being finished, leaving a wider space for the tree to fall. The previous banner was removed, replaced with another saying:

Tree Felling Commencing today

Drivers moved the two feller buncher machines into the barricaded area and parked on both sides of the oak tree.

"Oh no! This is just so terrible!", Gogzy squealed.

"They've left the cutting machines right beside the Tree of Life."

She couldn't cheer herself up.

"Where's Querciabella, Gagzy?", she yelled.

"I'm sorry?" Sophia replied, puzzled.

"Who is Querciabella?"

"It's ok, Sophia.", Said Gagzy.

"She's a girl we know, but I don't see her today. I don't think she's here. Come on Gogzy. We mustn't give up hope. Let's get on with the protest. Set up the table here, near that sign about tree felling.

That's it, and we'll put the two chairs beside the table with the petition pages and the pen attached to the clipboard for people to sign.

And look, there are more people arriving… And lots of kids from our school, carrying banners.

See what the banners say:

Love Nature   Save the Oak Tree   Save the Tree of Life."

"Love nature… Save the oak tree… Save the Tree of Life…", the school friends yelled in unison.

"Thanks, guys.", Gagzy waved and called back to them.

She leaned towards Gogzy while Sophia was busy fixing a badge on to her uniform, so the badge was visible to everyone.

Scottish Police   Security Officer

Those words told everyone who she was.

Look around you, Gogzy." Gagzy whispered in her sister's ear.

"Apart from the people, and the kids from our school, who do you see?"

"I see Misnich and lots of Pixies." Gogzy squeaked.

"So, we're not all by ourselves, here, Gogzy. Now where is mum's voice amplifier.

Ah, it's here at the bottom of my bag. And I have the petition poster mum printed for us. It's laminated, so I'll hang it on front of the table for all to see, just below the clipboard for people to sign."

We, the undersigned, oppose the developments taking place on Moreau Island. Stop the changes.

We oppose:

1. Building a hotel and golf course which will spoil the peace of the island.
2. Removing the ancient castle ruins.
3. Changing the flow of Moreau River to build chalets.
4. Removing otters and beavers which live on the riverbank. The riverbank is their home.
5. Chopping down the Oak tree, the beautiful Tree of Life, to make way for a hotel.

Please support our protest and sign the petition on the clipboard.

More people were arriving and one or two approached as Gagzy secured the protest poster to the table. One of them spoke to Sophia.

"Excuse me Officer, what are those big machines beside the oak tree, the ones with the words *'Feller Buncher'*?"

"I believe they are machines which will be used to chop down the tree, sir. It's why the girls are protesting and asking people to sign a petition to stop it happening."

"Shocking!", said the man.

"My wife and I will sign your petition young lady.", he said turning to Gagzy, who was setting up the voice amplifier to address the growing numbers of people.

"Thank you, sir."

"Good morning, everyone." She spoke into the loudspeaker.

"It's great to see so many people are here to support our protest and see what's happening on Moreau Island.

I'm Gagzy and beside me is my sister, Gogzy.

We read in the newspaper about plans to change the island, and we decided it wasn't right.

It was unjust and unfair to the plants and animals to put profit and money before nature. We decided to start our own peaceful protest and that's why we're here today, hoping you will join us and sign our petition.

Please come forward and sign our petition!"

She shouted in her loudest yelling voice as more people came to the table, forming a queue to sign the petition.

"Look at this beautiful oak tree. It is one hundred and eleven years old.", Gagzy carried on speaking.

"It could live for hundreds of years more. But the developers want to make a lot of money, so, they want to chop it down using ugly feller buncher machines.

It's wrong. They just don't care. Yesterday they were capturing otters and beavers to take them away from their home in the river.

They tried to change the course of the river, pulling down plants, trees, and threatening birds and other small animals. But they failed. Nature stopped them building their dams, by sending a tornado yesterday. You must have heard it if you didn't see it. But look down at the seaside before you go home. You'll see what nature thinks of their greedy plans. That tornado sucked in all their machines and dumped them down on the beach.

And that's why they've turned their attention to this beautiful oak tree, the Tree of Life. They plan to chop it down today." Gagzy yelled with passion.

"Please join our protest. Please sign our petition! Sign our petition today!

And we want a Tree Protection Order, that's a T.P.O., for short. There isn't much time to get it, but if we do, we might be able to stop this happening today.

Save our tree. Save the Tree of Life."

"Well done, Gagzy and Gogzy."

There were calls from their school friends and all the people queueing up to sign the petition.

"You were brilliant. You've made a great start, Gagzy." Gogzy said with feeling and admiration of her older sister.

"Look at the length of the queue of people waiting to sign."

But just as things were starting to go well, two people stood before them at the table. They were the man in the stripy suit and the lady with the glossy, red lipstick.

"You two yet again!", the lady with the glossy, red lipstick snarled.

"I've told you what will happen if you keep interfering. Dark dungeons await you! Do you hear me? Dark dungeons await you!"

"You have no right to stick your noses into our business.", said the man in the stripy suit.

But he was wrong. They hadn't noticed officer Sophia standing nearby. She was quick to step forward. Her uniform and her Scottish Police badge made them take a step backwards.

"Are you making threats against a lawful and peaceful protest?" She asked the lady with the glossy, red lipstick.

Gagzy reacted before the lady could reply, and Gagzy told the truth.

"She said she would put us in the castle dungeons where the ghosts are if she sees us here again."

"Did you? Did you threaten these girls who have organised a lawful and peaceful protest?" Sophia asked the lady with the glossy, red lipstick.

"I thought they were making a nuisance of themselves. I thought they had stolen the keys to our trucks. I was just trying to scare them off, officer. I never intended to put them into the dungeons."

"Did you steal any keys, Gagzy and Gogzy?"

Gogzy was about to answer…

"It wasn't us; it was…"

But before she could say it was the Pixies who took the keys, Gagzy jumped in, just in the nick of time.

"It was one of their workers who dropped his keys. Someone must have found them lying on the ground. We were up here on the hill, nowhere near the missing keys."

"I see."

Sophia turned again to the lady with the glossy, red lipstick and the man in the stripy suit.

"I should remind you this is a lawful protest and children with a complaint have equal rights to protest.

I am a Police officer and I'm here to ensure this right is protected. You may continue with your announcements, Gagzy."

At that moment Gogzy wanted to jump up and down shouting *'yippee!'*, but she stopped herself.

"Save the Tree of Life! Support our petition!" Gagzy yelled in her loudest voice, while the man in the stripy suit, and the lady with the glossy, red lipstick went away with their tails between their legs. They had been given a ticking off by Constable Sophia.

While Gagzy was speaking, Gogzy watched Misnich and the Pixies. They stood on top of the feller bunchers jumping up and down, pulling at levers and gear boxes, trying to make the machines move away. But the Pixies had never seen such machines, and they failed in their efforts.

Then Gogzy saw someone approach the barricade, someone she knew… It was Querciabella, carrying Cumhachd in her right hand, appearing as calm as she always did, and signalling to the Pixies to come away from the felling machine. They jumped from it and ran off, disappearing into the leaning turret.

"Gagzy, there's Querciabella. I'm going to speak to her."

"Which one is Querciabella, Gagzy?", Sophia asked, looking towards people arriving beside the barricades.

"I don't see her in the crowds, Sophia." Gagzy answered.

She knew she couldn't invite Sophia to meet Querciabella.

"Querciabella!", Gogzy called as she ran and tried to hug her, forgetting for an instant, that it wasn't possible.

She reached out and grasped only the breeze, the thin air surrounding Querciabella.

Her eyes blinked in confusion.

"Gogzy!", exclaimed Querciabella.

"Aren't you forgetting? We see and hear each other. But we may never make contact. We're in different dimensions, and the boundaries are closed to each other. I'm sorry, but alas, touching is impossible."

"Sorry, I was so excited to see you. And you know what's happening here, don't you, Querciabella." She said squeakily and a little tearfully.

"I do, Gogzy. But please, shed no tear. What will be, will be. I hear Gagzy. She fights a brave fight with her words. Your defence against the *'big folk'* is strong. Let's go to her. I will stand beside her while you sit again at the table, and the lady with you, she won't know I'm there."

"Ok."

Gogzy returned to her table to speak to Sophia, and

Gagzy welcomed Querciabella with a smile and listened as she spoke.

"Thank you, Gagzy for supporting our cause. Your words have power and strength. But I must tell you this. If the tree-cutting machine does its work, you and Gogzy will witness what happens to me. Others around you will see only the fate of my Oak tree.

Misnich and his friends have left, so, no one else will see what you will see. I must prepare you for what will happen.

When the branches come off the Tree of Life, you will see me fall to the ground."

"No!", Gagzy gasped.

"But you have Cumhachd to defend you, Querciabella."

"Cumhachd cannot enter the world of the *'big folk'*, Gagzy. She cannot switch dimensions in my defence.

You will see my pain. I cannot hide that from you. If this is to be, then so it must be. Comfort each other by knowing you have fought a brave fight for a just cause.

If my mighty oak tree falls, you will see me vanish. I will be gone. But I ask you, please don't weep for me. I will return through another acorn. It is the way of the Tree of Life."

Gagzy fought back tears, helped by the interruption of a stranger at the table, asking if he could write a comment beside his signature.

"What will you write, sir?", she asked.

"I'm writing… *'To fell this oak tree is a crime against nature.'*

Suddenly there were cries and boos from people gathered around the barricades.

"Shameful… Disgraceful… Stop this destruction of life… booo… boooo…"

Drivers entered the cab of the feller bunchers and were gearing up the engines.

The machines' tracker bases began to roll as they moved closer to the tree, raising long, cranelike arms, with buncher grippers rising high, to snap and bunch the branches on both side of the tree.

There was a short silence as people stood by awaiting what now seemed sure to happen.

Amid the silence, a voice was heard, calling…

"Stop… Stop… Stop!"

Gagzy heard the cries in the distance.

"Someone wants them to stop, but the feller bunchers are about to start crunching up the branches, Gogzy. It's too late!"

"Stop what you're doing!" Gagzy ran forward, screaming at the drivers.

"Someone is coming. He wants you to stop."

But the engines had started to roar, and the drivers heard nothing. Gagzy's yells were drowned out.

Suddenly, instantly, the wind direction changed, and its force turned to whirling gale-force. The long arms of the feller bunchers were caught in a powerful gust. It spun them full circle till they faced away from their target, the Tree of Life.

"Blustering blasts!", exclaimed Gagzy, who was blown towards the table where Gogzy stood with Querciabella and Sophia.

"What just happened, Gogzy?"

"I don't know, Gagzy, but I can make a guess." She whispered, as Sophia stood beside them.

"I bet it's Anemone, blowing an angry blast of wind at the fennel bunchers for trying to harm Querciabella."

Querciabella nodded and smiled towards the sisters. They alone heard her words.

"Anemone blows as she will, as gently as a breeze, or as fierce as a tempest."

The gale calmed as a man rushed forward, arriving on the hilltop just as the long arm of the machines swung back into position.

He spoke through a loudspeaker, in a voice much louder than the sound from Gagzy's voice amplifier.

"Stop what you are doing, at once."

A man in a grey suit appeared from amid the crowds. He carried a Tannoy loudspeaker.

He moved a section of the barricade, entered the area where the fennel bunchers were about to start work, and spoke to both drivers.

"You must stop what you are doing. A Tree Protection Order has been requested for this oak tree. I'm from the Tree Protection Council. Until a decision is made, I am stopping the felling of this tree. A police officer is present, so, should you doubt what I'm saying, she will confirm it is correct.

Now, drivers, I must ask you to step down from the cabs of the feller bunchers."

The crowds cheered, as the drivers switched off the engines and stepped down from the control cabins.

"Yes, yes, yes!" Gagzy yelled into her amplifier.

"Yippee! Yippee! Yippee!" Gogzy jumped up and down, excited and delighted.

Querciabella remained calm, and Sophia walked off to speak to the man in the grey suit.

"We've done it, Gogzy. Mum's advice has done it! She must have spoken to the Tree Protection Council. We've done it, Querciabella!"

But Querciabella had moved, and Gagzy turned to see her walk into the Tree of Life, knowing she was safe for now.

She turned to Gogzy.

"Gogzy, Querciabella has gone back into her tree. She didn't say anything! Did she know all along what would happen?"

"Maybe Gagzy, maybe Whitewave told her."

"It's a mystery, Gogzy, because she talked as though she didn't know, but she walked away as though she wasn't surprised!

Anyway, how many names have signed the petition?"

"I've just been counting. There are three hundred and seventeen names on the clipboard, and the online petition has seventeen hundred and fifty-seven signatures, and it's increasing every hour."

"Amazing. It's starting to look like we're winning. All we need is for that man with the loudspeaker to come back and tell us the T.P.O. has been granted, and the tree can't be touched."

"It's brill, Gagzy!"

Just as they were feeling happy and uplifted, the next person in the queue to sign the petition stood before the sisters at the table.

She had sneaked into the queue unnoticed, while Sophia was speaking to the man with the loudspeaker. It was the lady with the glossy, red lipstick. She was scowling, wrinkling her nose and pursing her big red lips, before snarling at the girls.

"It's all your fault! I'll see you in the dungeons, yet. I will."

"How is it all our fault? We didn't make the tornado, did we?", Gagzy argued back.

"I know you two!", she growled in a whisper.

"Look at you with your silly jackets. What's that embroidery around the edges? You're bad luck, you two. I've heard everything about you and your faeries, goblins, witches and warlocks… You talk to Gnomes and faeries, and I want to know how you do it. You'll tell me how it's done after a spell in the dungeons. Don't think you're getting away with this. The dungeons are where the nastiest demons and goblins are hiding, waiting for you… And the ghosts… Yes **ghosts!** Just you wait and see those ghostsssss…!"

She hissed as she said the last part of that word. She searched for a look of fear in their faces and found it in in Gogzy's eyes.

"Ghosts can't harm humans!", Gagzy yelled back at her.

"And we love our jackets, with their Celtic embroidery. Maybe you should look at your face in the mirror. Your red lipstick is all smudged."

"Give me that clipboard! I'll sign your petitionsssss…!" She hissed again, before grabbing the clipboard and writing something rapidly on the space for the next signature, then she darted away before Sophia spotted her.

"What did she write, Gogzy?" Gagzy asked.

"It says… *'Trees are a waste of good space. Chop the thing down!'*

But she didn't sign it, Gagzy."

"She wouldn't give herself away. That's all, Gogzy. She's just not nice. She wants to scare us. Don't be put off by what she said. Today is a big success, but we haven't won yet. The victory will come when mum tells us the developers are getting their money back, their plans have been cancelled, and the Tree Protection Order has been granted. All these signatures will be a massive help."

Sophia returned to the table with the man in the grey suit, who spoke to them.

"Well done, you guys! You should be proud of yourselves. What a job you've done! You're a great example to kids everywhere. You've shown you can protest as strongly as any grown-up person.

The first time I saw a 100-year-old oak tree being chopped down… it was horrible… A giant work of nature wasted in its prime, after growing for a hundred years, and it could have lived for hundreds more.

People are still queuing up to sign your petitions. May I take a screen shot of the signatures please. It will help with the decision to grant the Tree Protection Order."

"Please do.", said Gagzy.

"There's just one nasty comment from a moment ago, but she didn't sign it. She was one of the developers who wants to remove the tree. It was the person you spoke to earlier, Sophia."

Sophia looked at the comment.

"She hasn't signed it, so it doesn't count. You can score out that entry, Gagzy."

The man in the grey suit took screen shots of all the signatures on the clipboard.

"I spoke to your mum on the telephone early today." He told them.

"I told her a final decision about the T.P.O. will be made in two days, that's Friday in a meeting at 11.00 a.m. So, if you keep your petition going until Thursday, and ask your mum to send me screenshots of all the signatures early on Friday morning, I think you have a great chance of the T.P.O. being granted. I should be going now. So, good luck, girls."

"Thank you very much, sir."

"When do you want to go home?" Sophia asked.

"Let's head off now, Gogzy." said Gagzy.

"We've had a great day."

"Ok, Gagzy."

"Ok. I will leave with you.", said Sophia.

"I see people are already starting to leave with smiles on their faces. It has been a great day's work for you, Gagzy and Gogzy."

"Thanks, Sophia."

Inside the Dungeons

After the day of the Protest, the sisters slept in their tree house.

Each had a little bedroom under the branches, where they were allowed to sleep during summer holidays.

"Are you awake, Gagzy." Gogzy called from her room.

"Nearly…" Gagzy answered, still dozing in a half-slumber.

"The rustle of the leaves around my room just woke me. I had a nightmare, Gagzy."

"What about?", Gagzy asked with a wobbly voice.

"It was the lady with the glossy, red lipstick. She was there in my dream with her big growly face. She shoved me onto the top step leading down into the dungeons. I could see you were already down there, and you had your torch. She kind of nudged me with her shoulder, and said…

'Get down those stairs and play hide-and-seek with the ghosts. Ha! Ha! Ha! Ha! Ha!'

She screeched and cackled, Gagzy. That's what she did in my dream. She nudged me, screeching and cackling… right in front of my face, she was! Her dark eyes stared right into me and her big red lips were pouting. They pouted right in front of me, while the skin on her nose wrinkled!"

Gogzy shrieked, like she was still in her dream.

"Don't worry about it, Gogzy." Gagzy sounded more awake.

"She was trying to look like a witch when she made that face. And remember what mum told us about dreams. They're just what your brain does to make sense of things that happened the day before."

"Yes, but it was so real. And we've had dreams like that before, where they turn out to be true, Gagzy!"

"Dreams are like that, Gogzy. They always seem real."

Gagzy came into Gogzy's room.

"It's ten o'clock. I think we should go back on the eleven o'clock boat, try for more signatures, and just see what's happening with everything. I'll bring my torch, just in case your dream comes true, ok?"

"Ok, Gagzy."

"Querciabella's tree is safe for now, and so is Whitewave's river, and so are the animals on the riverbanks.

The developers are probably still tidying stuff up after Anemone dumped the machines onto the beach. So, I wonder what their plans are now, Gogzy.

But I better wash my face before we go anywhere."

The 11.00 o'clock boat was waiting with only two people on it.

"Maybe we won't get many signatures, today, Gagzy."

Gogzy spoke as they sat on the boat.

"Maybe, Gogzy. It's easy for people to sign the online petition, so they might not bother to travel. But we can still check what those developers are doing now. I bet they're annoyed at us for interfering."

They alighted from the boat and walked along the cliffside towards the river and the castle ruins at the top of the hill.

"Things are quieter than yesterday, Gogzy"

"Much quieter, Gagzy." Gogzy agreed.

They climbed the hill to see changes were underway, and the first person they met was the man with the blue dungarees.

"Ahah…", he said keenly.

"So, you're back. And where's your police lady friend today?" He asked.

"She's not coming today." Gogzy told him.

"We only had her for one day. She was there so no one could stop our protest. Why is everything so quiet? And why are they moving all the tents away?"

"Well, the bosses have decided on a new plan. With all the mess after the tornado, we can't carry on with the work on the river. And, with us not allowed to go near the oak tree, we're moving the tents nearer to the woodland bit of the island."

"So, what work will you be doing instead?", Gagzy asked.

"I'm not sure yet, but I think they've changed their plan to build a golf course. Something weird keeps happening on the golf course. The holes for the golf balls… They keep filling themselves in again! Someone must be creeping around in the night when everyone's asleep and plugging those holes!

And the big Marquee tent, it keeps falling… No sooner has it been erected… it falls again! It just collapses! And it was supposed to be our cafeteria.

Is it you, maybe? Are you filling in the holes and pulling down the Marquee? Surely you girls wouldn't do that."

"No way!", exclaimed Gagzy.

"We go home at night."

"One of our bosses thinks it might be you."

"Which one?" Gagzy asked.

"I might lose my job if I tell you."

"Ok, well... We'll tell you, because we know who it is, don't we Gogzy."

"Yes. It's the lady with the glossy, red lipstick." Said Gogzy, boldly.

"I bet she blames us."

"How did you know?" He asked.

"We know stuff." Gagzy answered with a smile.

"But what work will you do now, if you have to stay away from the river and the oak tree?"

Gagzy was keen to know the answer, and this man with the blue dungarees was friendly, much friendlier than both the lady with the glossy, red lipstick, and the man with the stripy suit.

"Well for now... It's the dungeons.", he answered.

"We've started work on the dungeons. But there's more to be done down there.

First, I'm guessing the plan is to build a holiday camp in the woodland, with lots of amusements, close to the sea where kids like you can play on the beach. And the dungeons will be here as a scary tourist attraction.

And, we'll have to chop down more trees in the woodland... But they won't be oak trees. But listen, I'm not sure what will come next. I'm guessing. I'm not a boss."

"You should tell your bosses not to go into the woods."

Gogzy spoke in a serious voice, and her worried face told him no one should go into the woods.

"There's something bad in there. Don't go deep inside the woods. Stay close to the Tower house. It's ok there."

"We won't have a choice about that. We need to go deep inside the trees, so we're closer to the sea and the beach where kids can play."

"There's something dark, ancient, and scary in there. We've been told this by someone who knows about it." The man in the blue dungarees must have sensed Gogzy's fear, but he didn't show it.

"Well, it can't be much worse than what's been happening at this end of the island. Some of the guys are starting to think this island is jinxed. Is it? Is it jinxed?"

"We don't know that." Gagzy told him.

"It's just… Well, we've heard stories that something **very** bad is in those woods. And we've been told to stay away. We are to stay well away from there."

"Ok, but I'll keep that to myself. If I spread news like that, no one will want to work in the woods. Enjoy your visit. I best get on with moving these tents. The dungeons will need to wait. We're off to the woods."

The man with the blue dungarees returned to where the tents were being taken down.

A troubled look stayed on Gogzy's face.

"He didn't want to hear what we told him, Gagzy. He probably thinks we're just kids imagining daft stuff. But he should have listened to us. If they go into those woods, they could disturb the Dark Elemental."

She shuddered as she said the words.

But Gagzy was excited.

"At least we tried to warn him, Gogzy.

But listen, he said he wasn't sure, and that he was guessing about a holiday camp, but he wasn't guessing when he said they couldn't work on the river or go near the oak tree. That's what they've been told by the bosses… To stay away from the river and the oak tree. This is brilliant news!"

"Yippee! Your right, Gagzyy. It's terrific! We've really helped Querciabella and Whitewave too. That is so good.

And he said some of the guys think the island is jinxed. That's good too. Maybe they'll get fed up and just go home!"

"Maybe, Gogzy, but look, something's going on over by the trapdoors into the dungeons. The doors are open. Quickly, let's hide behind the Oak tree and watch.

It's the lady with the glossy, red lipstick and a man. They're picking up those bags and carrying them downstairs into the dungeons."

"What's in those bags, Gagzy?"

"There are ten bags, Gogzy, with writing on the sides. But it's too far to see the words. That's the last one going downstairs now.

And the man he's coming back up, and he's walking away."

"I see him, Gagzy. So, where's the lady with the glossy, red lipstick, and what has she done with those bags?"

Before Gagzy had time to answer, they heard voices coming from inside the trapdoors… Loud angry voices.

"Get away from me. I'm finished with this."

It was a lady's voice they didn't recognise.

"Come back here."

A second woman called aloud.

There was silence till a woman they hadn't seen before stepped out of the trapdoor entrance, before running across the clearing, waving her arms frantically, and screaming.

"Get me away from here! Get me away from here! I'm not going back down there again. I won't work in there anymore."

"Are you ok?" Gagzy called to her.

But before the woman could answer, someone else appeared at the top of the dungeon stairs and stepped into the clearing.

It was the lady with the glossy, red lipstick, and she was chasing the woman.

"What are you afraid of, Katy?" She called to her.

"I saw it… That face with no body… I saw it laughing at me. I won't go back down there."

"What you saw was just a scary prop. That's all it was."

"That was no prop!" Katy answered, shrieking.

"I made those props and that wasn't one of them, because it had no eyes. All my props had eyes; they had fake eyes."

"The eyes must have fallen out.", said the lady with the glossy, red lipstick.

"Those eyes couldn't have fallen out, because they were all stuck in with superglue. They were fixed fast with the strongest superglue… And that thing I saw, it was laughing at me, and it was floating round a corner, and it didn't have a body. All the ones I made were props fixed to the walls. I'm leaving here, and I'm not coming back! I'll find another job where bodyless heads don't laugh at people who work there."

With those words, Katy rushed off to take the first boat back to the mainland.

While they were arguing, Gagzy was as curious as she always was. She tip-toed towards the open trapdoors and took one step down, peering into the darkness where candles flickered, throwing a shadowy light around the interior.

She saw enough to know there was no floating head. Her curiosity tempted her to take another step, then another step, then another… down into the dungeons. She took the torch from her backpack and shone it into a passage leading away from the last step, the thirteenth step on the stairs

The lady with the glossy, red lipstick didn't see anyone else until Katy had run too far for their argument to continue.

But then she spotted Gogzy, who panicked and ran towards the trapdoors, calling for Gagzy.

"Gagzy!" She screamed from the ground above.

"Come back out of there!"

Suddenly, Gogzy realised the lady with the glossy, red lipstick was standing right behind her, and she turned to see the pouting red lips on the big, growly face, leering at her from dark eyes.

"Gagzy!" She screamed again.

But there was no time for Gagzy to get back. She had moved away from the bottom of the stairs.

And everything that happened next happened very fast.

The lady with the glossy, red lipstick whispered in Gogzy's ear, an eerie whispering which made her words sound even more scary than if she said them aloud.

"The locks on these trap doors open and close automatically. They'll open again in two hours. In the meantime, I've set you a little challenge."

She whispered softly, and Gogzy felt hot breath touch the skin on her cheeks.

"I know nasty little kids like you love a challenge. So, get into the dungeons with your sister and visit the prison cells. See what's inside. It's a fun little challenge for you."

She stopped her eerie whispering.

"Maybe a good scare will stop you sticking your noses into other people's business!"

She added loudly and angrily, her voice now booming into Gogzy's right ear.

Then she nudged her shoulder causing her to take a few steps down, and as she did so, Gogzy heard her say the words from her own dream!

'Get down those stairs and play hide-and-seek with the ghosts. Ha! Ha! Ha! Ha! Ha!'

She screeched and cackled.

Gogzy was back in her dream as the trapdoors slammed closed behind her. It would be two hours till they opened again. She had no choice but to step down to the bottom of the thirteen steps, which led into a long, shadowy passage with prison gates on either side.

"Gagzy, look what you've done to us!", she yelled, her voice echoing into the dungeon darkness.

"Oh no! Now we're trapped in here and only that horrible lady with the glossy, red lipstick knows where we are. She saw us and she pushed me down here, just like in my dream, Gagzy."

"*Oooooooooooooooooaaaaaaghhh!*" A scream echoed along the length of the passageway.

"Ignore that, Gogzy. It's a sound effect. It's just a prop they've put in to scare and amuse visitors... Look, I'm sorry, Gogzy. I am. I'm sorry. I just couldn't stop myself. Curiosity killed the cat; I just hope it doesn't do the same to us!"

"Don't say that Gagzy!"

"I couldn't stop myself stepping downstairs!", Gagzy said again.

"If there really was a floating head with no body and no eyes, and it was laughing, I wanted to see it. I just needed to see if it was real. That's all."

"Did you see it?", Gogzy asked in a squeaky voice.

"No, but I suppose it could be hiding somewhere else."

"But why wouldn't you be scared to see a floating head with no body? How could you **not** care about that?

I would be screaming terrified, Gagzy, just like that lady, Katy."

Gogzy yelled, her voice now screeching, and echoing along the path which lay before them.

"Gogzy, you must calm down. Don't I keep telling you? Ghosts are only there in shape. You can see them, but they can't harm you. We can see them because of our special gifts. But they can't touch us because they're in another dimension. Just like you couldn't shake Querciabella's hand, because she's in another dimension.

If nasty ghosts tried to touch us, they would just be thrown right back to where they came from, because they are nasty. So, calm down."

Gagzy gave her younger sister a warm hug.

"Well, why wasn't Querciabella thrown back into her dimension, Gagzy?"

"Because Querciabella is a good guy, and a Force of Nature. There's nothing nasty about her.

But listen, we're in here now, so we better figure out a way to get out. Let's walk ahead and see where it leads. There are flickering candles, and I have my torch. At least we're not stuck in total darkness. Or maybe we should go back first and check the trapdoors. They might be open."

"No, she told me... The lady with the glossy, red lipstick... She told me the trapdoors were locked for two hours. We can't get out for two hours."

"Then we better find another way."

"My dream came true, Gagzy. She nudged me down those stairs, just as I told you."

"So, how did your dream end, Gogzy?"

"I don't know. I woke up just as the trapdoors slammed closed behind me, and we were left standing in here with you shining your torch. So, what if we can't find a way out? It's horrible and I'm terrified in here." She screeched.

"There must be another way out. Lots of castles with dungeons had secret passages and secret ways of escaping from attackers. We'll just keep walking down this pathway."

Gogzy calmed down at the thought there might be a way out. She peered into the distance, her eyes following the beam of Gagzy's torch.

It wasn't an even walkway ahead, and she saw the passage wasn't built by human diggers.

It was more like the passage of a cave, an underground tunnel with bumps, humps, and hazardous holes on walls and on the ground… Features which had always been there.

'How old is this place?' The question popped into Gogzy's head.

Her sixth sense told her they were in a place which was as old as the earth itself.

Ancient builders had built the castle on top of it. But they hadn't built the caves.

Her awareness was finely tuned, her senses alert to every detail of sound, light, smell, and touch.

Gogzy was hyper-aware, and suddenly her brain rushed into overdrive.

She caught sight of shadowy movements on walls. She heard bangs and thuds in the distance, sounds which echoed along the tunnel.

She smelled a whiff of foul air wafting past her sniffing nostrils.

Her ears alerted to sounds of flowing water, spilling and splashing as it fell.

Something touched her shoulder. Was it someone's hand? Was it the wing of a bat or a bird? Was it solid or ghostly?

Was it alive or dead?

"Gagzy, we must get out of here. We must find a way out of here!" She yelped in a high-pitched squeak.

"That nasty lady with the glossy, red lipstick… She told me she's set us a challenge… To look inside every prison cell. That must be the rooms with the iron gates we see along the sides of this tunnel. They might help us find a quick way out. But… They might not!

Oh no! We'll **never** find a way out. We won't, Gagzy! We'll **never** find a way out! We're trapped!"

Gogzy was in a panic.

"Calm down, Gogzy… Don't panic, that won't help. Look, over there on the right side of the tunnel, there's a curved little corner in the wall and there's something inside it."

Gagzy shone her torch into the corner.

"Let's check it out."

Gogzy tried to calm herself.

"It's the ten bags, Gagzy. They have hidden them in here. They're split into two bundles of five.", she said, her voice shaking.

"See the writing on the bags, Gogzy. One bundle says, **'Zinc Phosphide',** and the other is **'Warfarin'**. And both say they are poisonous. I wonder what they are for."

Gogzy composed herself.

"I'm not sure, Gagzy. But I think they might be chemicals."

"So, why would the lady with the glossy, red lipstick be hiding poisonous chemicals in here, Gogzy.? Maybe we'll find out more about that later."

"Yikes! Look, Gagzy… Up ahead, at the next corner on the left… Did you see it? Did you see it, Gagzy?"

"What? I didn't see anything. I was looking at the bags of poison. What did you see?"

"Oh no! I hope it isn't just me who's seeing these things! Oh no!"

Gagzy switched her torch to its brightest beam.

"Quick, tell me, Gogzy. What did you see?"

"Stop here. I don't want to go along there, Gagzy."

"Ok, we'll stop, but what did you see?"

Gogzy stopped walking and froze on the spot where she stood. It was hard to stay calm.

"Remember what we read in the newspaper, or was it the book in the library? We were reading about terrors and torments in this place."

She spoke in a whisper.

"Remember how it said the skeleton had its feet chopped off for running away, trying to escape. Then we read about hands being chopped off of anyone who was caught stealing food. Well… That's what I just saw… Oh no! I know what I saw, Gagzy… I just saw a pair of hands floating out of the room on the left… And… And… And… Those hands… They were carrying a bowl filled with eggs, Gagzy! It's like… Those hands were stealing the eggs! And there were no arms attached to the hands! There wasn't even a body… Just hands… Oh no! We've got to get out of here. Gagzy! I can't stay here for another minute! And I've just remembered something Querciabella said. She said Misnich and his friends loved the history hidden in the castle's ancient walls… The ghosts and phantoms who linger there, hidden in the realm of the mysterious. That's what she said, Gagzy."

She had stopped whispering.

"It means Querciabella knew there **were** ghosts here.", she yelled at the top of her voice and the echo boomed down the long pathway.

"But Querciabella and the Pixies weren't afraid of them, Gogzy. Try to remember the golden rule… Ghosts can't hurt us humans."

"Aaaaaggghhhaaaaa!" Someone screamed.

"Yikes! Someone's screaming again!"

"Ignore it, Gogzy. It's another prop, a pretend scream. That's what those developers have been doing in here. That's the start of their work in the dungeons. It's what the man in the blue dungarees told us. He said they had made a start on the dungeons. They've been setting things up to make them scary for tourists who like to be scared. It's daft, but some people think it's fun to be scared. That's why they come for a day out. They get excited being scared in a scary place like this. Come on. Let's see if we can find that pair of hands.

And look, this is my medal from the Kingdom of the Fae. I've pulled it out from under my top. You do the same and we'll be protected. Nothing nasty will come near us while our medals are there, shining. Ok? Now, let's move forward and check that room on the left. You'll feel better when you see there's nothing but dust floating around in there. Come on, now. Whatever we see, don't run away, in case we get split up, or we run down some pathway and get lost. Just count to ten if you see something scary."

Gogzy stepped forward, gingerly, with Gagzy leading the way till they stopped at the entrance to the room, the prison cell on the left.

But it wasn't a dungeon cell with iron bars blocking its entrance. This one looked different from the ones with iron gates.

There was a soiled sign, ragged around its edges, hanging above the remains of a rotting wooden door. The sisters could just make out the words…

Dungeon Kitchen…

Handwritten, using some ancient quill pen.

Gagzy pushed open the creaking old door.

"See, Gogzy. The sign says this was once a kitchen. Maybe that's why you saw a bowl of eggs. It doesn't look much like a kitchen now. It just looks like a cave. It's a big gaping hole in the wall. But it must have been a kitchen at one time."

"But why were armless hands carrying a bowl of eggs, Gagzy?"

Gogzy was still whispering, in semi-darkness, amid echoes of dripping water.

"The owner of those ghostly hands must have been stealing the eggs before being caught. And the thief must have done it hundreds of years ago, and had his hands chopped off, Gagzy."

"Maybe. But look around you, Gogzy. There's no sign of any other food in here. And there's no sign of a bowl of eggs or floating hands.

So, count to ten, it might calm you down, then let's move on and see what's happening further down the tunnel."

"Ok." Gogzy counted to ten.

They tramped further into the tunnel, into the shadowy darkness, but with enough light from flickering candles, and Gagzy's torch, to show this was a damp, dirty place, shaped and carved by nature.

The pathway was one filled with rocks, snags, pitfalls, and small streams of water, dripping and seeping from cave walls on either side. It certainly wasn't a path made by human beings.

"Those streams running down the walls must lead somewhere, Gogzy. Look, follow the beam of my torch. They join up further down the path. They form a bigger stream, and it looks like it spills downwards, like a waterfall. That's where the splashing sounds are coming from. We should remember that. It could help us find our way out.

But while we're here, watch where you put your feet. One of those holes in the ground might be very deep. I'll keep shining my torch along the path ahead, so we can spot any dangers.

Those developers haven't finished their work in here. It's too messy and dangerous for tourists. We're stuck inside caves, here, Gogzy… No doubt about that…

They weren't always dungeons. They only became dungeons when people of long ago turned the caves into prisons."

"There's a signpost coming up ahead, Gagzy. After that, it looks like prison cells on both sides, all with iron gates. And… and… It looks like those iron gates go on, and on, as far as the beam of your torch goes.

This challenge is a trick. The lady with the glossy, red lipstick is making us walk deeper and deeper into the darkness. We can't do that, Gagzy."

Again, Gogzy had stopped whispering. She was yelping!

"Ok, let's check out that signpost. Then we'll decide what to do next.

It's a sign for tourists, Gogzy. See what it says:

1. Your spine will be chilled by terrifying thrills.
2. Bell book and candle, you must not handle.
3. With hands that clap you will be in a flap.
4. Piles of bones bring wailing and moans.
5. Legless feet make a noisy retreat.
6. A bowl full of eggs brings the shaking of legs.
7. To the dead in the bed, you must not be led.

… Many more scares await those bold enough to complete this tour of the ancient dungeons of Moreau Castle.

"This is just an advert for tourists, Gogzy. It's just to get them in the mood, so they're scared and excited at the same time. We don't need to worry about any of that."

"But it's more than that for us, Gagzy.", Gogzy squealed.

"Because I've already seen that pair of hands with the bowl of eggs. And I felt my legs shake when I did. That wasn't a prop!

Number three on the list says… With hands that clap, you will be in a flap… Is that a prop?

And what's coming next? We better move on and find out. Will we ever get out of here, Gagzy?

Maybe we should just check another two or three cells then turn back."

Gogzy's thoughts were racing.

"Ok, let's check the first cell on the left. Keep cool."

They approached a gate ravaged by the red-brown rust of centuries, but still standing strong. They peered through a latticed grill of ancient bars to see…

Nothing…

Nothing, except the inside of the cell. A single candle, fitted by developers, shed some light, and Gagzy beamed her torch inside.

They saw writings and scratchings on craggy walls. There was no furniture to sit on… no bed to sleep on.

Inside the gate, three steps, worn and bevelled, led to the floor below, a floor with no shape, only holes and rocks spread across it.

There were no windows for fresh air to enter. A jutting bump on a wall might be used as a seat. The dank and clammy smell of mould filled that prison cell. Spiders' webs decked the prison walls.

"What a horrible place for a prisoner to live in, Gagzy. How could anyone sleep in there?"

"A poor prisoner might go mad stuck in there, Gogzy."

Gogzy had calmed down a little.

"So, Gogzy, we've had a good look into this cell, and there's no sign of hands stealing eggs, or floating, laughing heads. It's just an empty cell."

Gagzy was about to move to the next one when there was a sudden outburst of noise from inside the empty cell. They stared, searching for the cause, but saw nothing.

The cell was empty, but the din was deafening! They took a step back.

"What's going on, Gagzy."

Gogzy yelled above the raucous shrieks, and in a flash, she switched back to her state of alarm.

"Count to ten, Gogzy. We might find out."

What came next were piercing sounds so ear-splitting, they could almost see them! If sound could be seen, this was the place.

What they heard was a crazy mix of screaming, yelling, yapping, screeching, all jumbled up with babbling, gurgling, splashing, rumbling, banging and crashing.

It was sore on their ears. Gogzy covered hers and counted to ten.

But suddenly, all was silent… And they stood together in a sinister silence!

Was this just a prop that wasn't working properly?

Or was it something else?

If it was meant to be scary, it was succeeding!

"Is this a prop, Gagzy?", Gogzy screamed!

Gagzy was trying to make up her mind about that, but she was distracted by the sudden coldness.

They began to shiver as they stood beside the cell gate.

Gogzy reached only number three of her count to ten.

"What's that stinky stink?", she yelled, as a dirty smell filled the air.

"It's too stinky, Gagzy!"

"Squeeze the end of your nose, Gogzy, so you don't smell it. There might have been skunks in here, and they spray a stinky smell. And hold tight your medal, it will keep you safe."

Gogzy clasped the special Fae medal in her right hand.

Then the clapping began.

Pairs of hands without arms appeared on the sides of the walls, each hand clapping the other. It was an eerie clapping, one without any cheering.

It replaced the sinister silence.

Gogzy finished her count to ten.

"Come on, Gogzy, we've had enough of this. If this is a prop it will scare **all** the tourists away! Is it a prop?

Who cares?

It's crazy, it's freezing, and it stinks. Let's scoot!"

They dashed off, further down the tunnel.

"That hand clapping, Gagzy. That was real. I don't think it was meant for tourists. I think it was meant for us, because whatever was doing it… well, it knew **we** could hear the sounds. It **knew** we could see and hear into other dimensions!

And all that screaming… That was meant to scare us."

"You're right, Gogzy. It was toying with us! It was trying to make fun of us! I think it was laughing at us!

But it **didn't** scare us. Just keep telling yourself that. It did **not** scare us. We don't scare that easily, Gogzy. So, keep counting to ten and keep telling yourself that. It did **not** scare us! Ok?"

"Ok, Gagzy. It did **not** scare us."

"It was just a bunch of clapping hands, Gogzy. What's scary about that?

But now, we must find a way out."

As Gagzy said those words a thought jumped into her head.

'Are these caves haunted?'

She couldn't make up her mind.

They hurried on to the next cell, which unlike the others had no gate with iron bars.

Gagzy shone her torch into the space.

A flat rock jutted out of a wall, and resting on it were a bell, a book and a lighted candle.

"A bell, a book and a candle… What's that all about, Gogzy?" Gagzy voiced her thoughts in puzzled tones.

"I don't know, but why are there no iron bars on this cell?", Gogzy answered.

"It's like it **wants** us to walk inside."

Gagzy took a step forward.

"Don't go in, Gagzy. Something isn't right about this…

A bell, a book, and a candle! It doesn't make any sense!"

Gogzy stood at the entrance to the cell. Gagzy took another step forward.

"Gagzy… One of the thrills on that notice we just saw… It said…

'Bell book and candle, you must not handle'.

"Don't touch anything in there, Gagzy. You must not handle anything."

Gagzy, being a risk taker, couldn't resist reaching forward to pick up that bell. But before her hand reached it, the bell jumped upwards and began to toll, a loud pealing toll.

It rung itself!

"Bonging bells!"

Gagzy jumped two steps back, but quickly, she stepped forward again, undeterred.

"What are you doing, Gagzy? We need to leave here. A bell can't ring by itself."

But Gagzy had entered her own zone of curiosity, and her hand reached towards the book.

"Don't touch it, Gagzy!", Gogzy yelled from the entrance to the cell.

But Gagzy didn't get the chance to touch it. As her hand reached out, the bell tolled again and the pages of the book began to turn, one by one, faster and faster, till they reached the end, before turning backwards, faster and faster, towards the beginning of the book.

Gagzy jumped away, taking another step back.

But again, she wasn't deterred.

She stepped forward a third time, towards the lighted candle, and reached out as though to pick up the candlestick.

"Oh no!" Gogzy yelled.

"Something feels bad about this! Whatever you're doing, don't do it. What are you doing, Gagzy?"

Gagzy's hand didn't reach the candlestick.

The bell tolled again, the loudest, longest toll, the pages of the book flipped and skimmed at rapid speed, sending air currents into the flame causing it to erupt as high as the roof, lighting up the whole cell.

Gogzy screamed.

"Aaaaaaagggghhhhhh! Oh No!"

Gagzy darted back to her side.

"It's ok! I was just fooling around. There's no harm done."

"Look up, Gagzy!" Gogzy screamed, cupping her cheeks in her hands.

"Up there in the corner of the roof."

Looking down at them was a face with no body! A face without eyes! And it was laughing!

"Ha! Ha! Ha! Ha! Ha! Ha!" It cackled.

"Make a run for it, Gogzy." Even Gagzy was spooked,

and they darted, away from the cell.

They tripped and stumbled as they ran, far and deeper into the dungeons, until

they stopped to take their bearings.

"Where are we, Gagzy. Are we lost?" Gogzy asked, rubbing a bruise on her knee where she had fallen.

"I don't know. Was it a prop?", Gagzy spoke, as though she was asking herself the question!

"That scary face we just saw… It must be the one the lady saw… Katy, the one who ran away… The fright has left me confused, Gogzy. I just don't know what to think any more!

And I'm not sure where we are, so, we must take care we aren't getting lost in here.

We ran in a straight line. We didn't turn any corners.

I'll turn my torch to its brightest beam. Heh! Look ahead, Gogzy. See how far those prison gates stretch into the distance. They go on as far as the beam of my torch, and on both sides! I don't think we should walk any further. What's the time?"

She checked her watch.

"We've only been in here about 30 minutes. That's another 90 minutes till those trap doors open. And look, Gogzy, we're on a downward slope. We've been running downhill, deeper underground. This isn't good. Where might we end up?"

"Look back from where we came, Gagzy. Shine the torch back."

Gagzy did so.

"See. We've been walking down hill since we came through the trapdoor. We've been walking and running on a downward journey. At the start we were on the hilltop, where the castle ruins are. That must mean that right now, we're inside the hillside. And we know where the hillside leads. It leads down to the river. So, we aren't lost, Gagzy. We're just kind of stuck inside a big hole. All we need to do now, is find our way to an opening on the side of that hole, because the side of the hole must be the side of the hill."

"Good thinking, Gogzy.

You see, when you calm down you think much better. So, let's have a look around here."

To their right side was another prison cell. Gagzy shone the torch onto a notice which hung on the gate.

Piles of bones bring wailing and moans

Gagzy shone the torch to reveal a group of skeletons inside, some seated, some standing upright.

As the light of the torch shone on them, they began to wail and moan, as though the torchlight triggered them into action, howling, sobbing, groaning and moaning.

But the sisters were not fooled.

Gagzy shone the torch beam away from them and the cell fell silent.

"This is a definite prop, Gogzy. The light of the torch trips them into yelling. Let's move on."

"What's that running sound, Gagzy. Shine the torch back along the path. Is someone coming? Maybe they've sent people to find us."

"There's no one there, but I hear the footsteps."

Gagzy shone the torch through iron bars on the next cell, where a flight of stone steps led underground, and running rapidly down those steps were dozens of worn and dirty old shoes, tied up with thongs.

The wearers of those shoes were missing! The shoes were running by themselves with only feet inside them!

Feet were running without legs or bodies!

"Aaaaagggghhhh!" It was Gogzy, not a prop, who yelled.

"It's another of the scares on the tourist notice, Gagzy...

'Legless feet make a noisy retreat'.

It's the ghostly feet of prisoners who tried to escape. Their chopped off feet are still running, hundreds of years later. Maybe it's a prop. Is it?"

Gagzy didn't answer.

<<<<<<<<<< *'Is this a prop or not a prop?'* >>>>>>>>>>

The words of that question echoed in her head.

She just didn't know any more!

"Count to ten, Gogzy, and let's follow that sound of running water. Do you hear it?"

Gogzy counted to ten. She counted at speed!

"Yes, I hear it.", she answered making a hasty retreat from the running feet.

What scare would be next?

Gagzy turned the torch beam to a part of the wall to see the source of the streaming water. And it was more than a trickle, it was an outflow running into a bigger stream on the cave floor below.

"Let's follow that stream, Gogzy."

It flowed a short distance, growing wider as it did so, passing a few more cells before turning a corner into a crack, a fissure in the rocky wall.

"Gogzy, I think we've found something. I think we might be in luck."

"Me too, Gagzy. That gap in the wall. It's big enough for us to squeeze through. And I've just remembered something. There was a stream which flowed into a cave on the hillside. Maybe this is where it was going."

"Yes, but the flow is downwards, and beyond the space in the wall, it must become a waterfall. Water can't flow uphill. So how high is the wall on the other side?

Is it too high for us to drop down?

We just need to hope it's not too high, because it will be falling onto rock below. I'll go first, Gogzy."

"Don't go in if it's too big a drop, Gagzy. If it's too high, we can look for another crack."

Gagzy stuck her head and arm into the crevice to shine her torch below.

"I think it's ok for us, Gogzy." She pulled herself back out of the gap.

"It's a wee bit too high for you, but not for me. If I dangle my feet, they should almost touch the bottom. Then I can catch you, if you come through feet first.

We might get our feet wet. That's all.

The water falls onto a sloping path, but it's still inside the hillside with more rocky walls beside it. So, we should be ok.

If we follow the path downwards, the water will reach the outside and join up with the river. That's my guess, Gogzy. Are you ready to try?"

"Ok. Did you see any hands, feet, or laughing faces in there, Gagzy?

"Not one."

"What about noises and smells?"

"Just the sound of the water falling, and the smell of the caves."

"Ok, Gagzy, you go first."

"Take my torch, Gogzy, and drop it down to me before you come through."

Gagzy pushed herself through the crevice feet first, and Gogzy watched her disappear till she could see only her hands gripping the edge, then she heard a short splash as she landed.

"Here comes your torch, Gagzy."

Gogzy dropped the torch and pushed herself through, feet first, then she gripped the edge of the crevice space with her hands.

"I have a hold on your legs, Gogzy, so, just let go now."

Gogzy slid down while Gagzy broke her fall.

"Yippee!" She exclaimed as she landed.

"We're out of the haunted dungeons, I hope."

"I hope so too. But there are no candles where we are now, so we mustn't lose the torch. Look, I'll shine it down the pathway.

See how it goes down steeply, and it turns a corner further along. It turns left. That's where we're going. Most of the path isn't in water, so we won't get too wet. Let's head on down there. The flow of the water is getting faster. I think we might be nearly there."

They reached the left turn and stopped to check out the scene before them.

"I'm going to switch the torch off, just for a second, Gogzy, to see if there is any chink of light ahead."

"Ok, Gagzy."

Gagzy switched the torch off for an instant, to look for a hint of daylight, but they stood in complete darkness.

"Turn it back on, Gagzy. I'm scared you might drop it in the darkness."

Gagzy switched it on again.

"See the pathway and the flow of the stream. It's on an even steeper downward slope. There can't be far to go. We're inside the hillside beside the river and that's where this stream is heading.

And look, in the distance, it turns right. Maybe there's a chink of light at that right turn. Let's head down there."

"Ok."

They carried on, their feet moving faster with the pull of the downward slope.

"Did you hear that, Gagzy? I thought I heard a voice, someone shouting."

"I wasn't sure, because of the ripple of the water. But we'll soon find out if we get closer, Gogzy."

Their footsteps quickened on the steep slope. They knew they must be close to a way out.

"Come back here!" A faint voice could be heard in the distance, and this time, both heard it clearly.

Then a dog barked, and in the excitement of hearing familiar sounds, Gagzy dropped the torch.

Gogzy panicked, engulfed in a sudden blanket of darkness.

"Switch it back on, Gagzy. I can't see a thing! It's pitch black! I can't see anything! I can't even see my fingers in front of my eyes. I need light! I need light! Help!"

Unnerved and agitated, Gagzy was flustered as she pawed around the pathway in search of the torch. Had it been carried away by the flow of the stream?

It hadn't. She grasped it on the edge of the waterside.

"I have it, Gogzy."

She switched on the light at the same moment as Gogzy released a shriek, a primal scream from deep within herself.

Standing before them was a terrifying image, a tall, shadowy spectre which made Gagzy jump backwards, pulling Gogzy by the arm, away from the wraith which stood before them.

It swung a chain with a spiky ball and brandished a mighty sword. It roared a full-throated growl.

It was the phantom gaoler.

Gagzy pulled Gogzy, so her sister stood behind her. She yelled defiantly at the ghost before them.

"Get away from us. You're not real. You can't harm us. Get back to where you came from! You're a nasty ghost. You're not real!"

But the vision stood, threatening, swinging the spiky ball, brandishing the huge sword, and growling like an angry bear.

"Get away! Get away! Get away!" Gagzy yelled again.

Then, seemingly from nowhere, a wonderful champion arrived on the scene.

The dog they heard barking came bounding along the pathway, passed the phantom, and spun around to place itself as a guard between it and the girls.

It growled ferociously, louder than the ghost.

It bared its teeth and angled its hindlegs, ready to pounce.

Incredibly, the ghost stepped backwards. Was it afraid? Had the dog frightened the ghost?

In that instant the dog leapt, attacking it.

But there was no moment of contact. Touching was impossible.

The phantom gaoler vanished. It was sucked into another dimension, one where it belonged.

And the dog who was their champion, the dog who rescued Gagzy and Gogzy was none other than Gugzy, the friendly Rottweiler.

"Gugzy!", the sisters squealed together.

"Yipee!" Gogzy jumped for joy.

"You saved us from that ghastly ghost."

Gugzy barked, jumping and licking their faces, bursting with excitement at seeing them again.

In that moment, Gagzy, Gogzy, and Gugzy were bonded as friends forever.

The happy threesome followed the rest of the pathway to the curve of the wall where they saw the light of day and left the dungeons.

Back Home

It was Friday morning, and the sisters slept late in their tree house bedrooms, exhausted after their ordeal trapped in the dungeons.

Gogzy jumped up first.

"Gagzy, look at the time. It's 10.30 already. This is the day when we find out if the Tree Protection Order is granted to save the Tree of Life, and Querciabella too. Mum is to phone the man this morning, remember."

"Oops…" Gagzy yawned.

"I was in the middle of a long dream. You, me and Gugzy were in a battle with that phantom gaoler. I'm just coming."

"I hope mum has good news for us, Gagzy. I'm scared thinking of what will happen to Querciabella if the developers are allowed to go ahead with those nasty plans for the tree."

"I know, but remember, Gogzy, you can't tell mum about Querciabella."

They pulled on jeans, tops, socks and trainers and scampered down the swinging rope ladder to find mum in the lounge, speaking on the landline.

She gave the sisters the *'thumbs-up'* sign as they entered the room.

"Thank you so much, sir. My daughters will be delighted at this positive outcome. Goodbye."

"It's good news! Yippee!" Gogzy jumped for joy.

"Yes! Yes! Yes!" Gagzy did three fist punches into the air.

"Yes, girls, your campaign to save the oak tree has been successful. A Tree Protection Order has been granted and the gentleman I just spoke to said he will send you a letter telling you the tree must not be damaged or harmed in any way, and a notice saying this will be placed beside the tree for all to see.

It will say:

THIS IS A TREE PROTECTION AREA.   KEEP OUT.

You will see it there when you return. So, Gabriella and Gloria, your protest has been a huge success… It's a job well done."

"Well done, you, mum. It was your brill ideas that helped us get there."

"Yippee!" Gogzy jumped for joy again.

"I can't wait to tell Qu…"

"Gogzy!" Gagzy interrupted.

"What were you about to say, Gogzy?" Mum asked.

"Oh, I was just about to say… I can't wait to tell, **quickly**, everyone who helped us with the protest, and signed the petitions, that they did a great job too."

"Any more news?" Mum asked.

"Yes, big news mum." Gogzy carried on talking.

"One of the developers, a lady with red lipstick… I don't think she liked me and Gagzy for doing the protest… She said we were interfering and sticking our noses into her business… And she set a challenge for us in the castle dungeons. She said we might like the scary things in there, because some kids think scary things are fun. Gagzy had already run ahead into the dungeons, then she pushed me in too. She told us to play hide and seek with the ghosts. She said it was a challenge, but she just wanted to scare us. So, we ended up stuck in there, because the trapdoors were locked for two hours."

"And they weren't real dungeons, Mum." Gagzy explained more.

"They were caves that had been turned into dungeons… Dark caves with some candles for light."

"Oh dear! Oh dear! Oh dear!"

Whenever mum said those words, the girls knew she wasn't pleased.

"I'm afraid I'll have to speak to your dad and police officer Sophia about this. Locking you inside dark dungeons by yourselves, challenge or not, it is **not** allowed."

"And that's not all, mum.", said Gagzy.

"Before we did the challenge, we saw her and a man carrying bags into the caves, ten bags, and we didn't know what they were. But when we were inside, we found them hidden in a corner.

I had my torch. The bags were stacked in two bundles of five. One bundle had the words *'ZINK PHOSPHIDE'*, and on the other, it said *'WARFARIN'*. Both bundles were marked as poisonous. Gogzy says those things are chemicals, but we don't know what they're used for. We think that lady with the glossy, red lipstick was up to something."

"Ok, let's do a quick check."

Mum picked up her smart phone.

"Oh dear! Oh dear! Oh dear!" She repeated the words which meant she didn't approve of something.

"What is it mum? Tell us." They spoke together.

"You won't like what I have to tell you."

"Tell us, please."

"It seems these chemicals may be used as poisons."

"Who are they meant to poison, mum?" Gogzy asked, alarmed.

"Did she want to poison **us**?", she screamed.

"No, Gloria, but they can be used as poisons to eradicate otters and beavers."

"What's *'eradicate'*?", Gagzy asked immediately.

"I'm sorry, but I think they would be used to kill the animals."

"What?" The sisters jumped out of their chairs.

"I knew that lady with the glossy, red lipstick was up to no good." Gagzy yelled at the top of her voice and stamped her feet.

"They must be planning to start on the river again, Gogzy. Once all the mess is cleared up after the tornado, they plan to poison the otters and beavers."

"Now calm down both of you. It's not that simple. It's not only trees which can be protected. Animals are also protected. And beavers and otters are among those which have the protection of the law. I'll speak to dad about this. He will make sure those hidden bags of poison are removed and confiscated. They won't be used to harm otters or beavers… And so… Phew…"

Mum sighed a relieved sigh, that she was able to calm her daughters, especially Gabriella, who looked at that moment as if she might explode with anger at the thought of poisoning innocent animals.

"Do you have any more news for me. Maybe some good news?"

"Yes, mum…", said Gogzy, more cheerfully.

"Great news. Did we tell you before about Gugzy?"

"Gugzy? I don't think so. Is that another nickname?"

"No, Gugzy is the dog we met on the island. He's a big Rottweiler, he looks fierce, but he loves us, and we've become besties. And we make a great team because his name is just like ours.", said Gogzy.

"So, what happened with Gugzy?" Mum asked.

Gagzy told the story.

"Well, we were stuck in the dark in those dungeons and trying to find a way out when we heard a dog bark just at the same moment as a monstrous phantom stood before us swinging a spiky ball and waving a big sword in front of us. The phantom was just one of the props in the dungeon…"

"Are you sure, Gagzy? I thought it was real." Gogzy interrupted.

"Well, whatever it was, it was scary, mum, and we had nowhere to run to. It was blocking our path, but just in the nick of time, Gugzy came bounding forward, growling fiercely at the phantom, and jumping onto it, he scared it off. It was Gugzy who came to our rescue. He made it vanish. He's our favourite dog friend now."

"Well, that is a good news story.", said mum.

"Well done, Gugzy. So, what's next for you now?" Mum asked.

"Can we go back tomorrow mum?", Gagzy asked.

"We want to see the notice saying the oak tree is protected. And will you tell dad about those bags of poison stuff? They're hidden in a corner in the dungeons. I want to be sure they can't be used to harm the animals living beside the river."

"I most certainly will.", Mum replied.

"And you can go back tomorrow. You will see the Tree Protection notice and probably Officer Sophia too. She will see to it that no rules are being broken."

Ignis, The Dark Elemental

After their chat with mum the sisters spent the rest of the day in their treehouse, playing computer games and chatting about adventures they remembered.

"Sometimes, Gagzy, I have nightmares about the sorcerer who sent us back one thousand years to the time of the Vikings. He was even scarier than the Vikings we met!"

"I know. My worst nightmare is about the time I was stuck inside the giant's boot, looking for the witch's spell book. I found it right inside the toe of the boot. And it was a dog who helped us that time too. It was Pooch, he sniffed out where the book was, and then you had to throw it into the fires of the witch's cauldron."

"That's when my angel came to help me, Gagzy. The flames were blazing high, and the spell book was just too heavy for my muscles to lift it right up. I heard my angel's voice inside my ear...

"Just a little higher, Gogzy".

"Gogzy, you were amazingly brave that day."

"But that phantom gaoler was just as terrifying, Gagzy. It appeared out of nowhere! Gugzy arrived just in time. Let's hope there will be no more scares tomorrow. I can't wait to see that sign saying:

Keep out, this is a protected area."

"Me too, Gogzy. And we'll find out if those bags of poison have been moved away. Maybe those developers will just give up and clear out. We'll find out tomorrow.

Next day, they left a little later than usual, getting the 12 o'clock boat.

It meant there was time for things to happen on the island, like moving the bags of poison, and the notice arriving about the protection of the oak tree.

They alighted from the boat, walked along the cliff edge and climbed the hill to find a busy scene.

Everyone was on the move. The tents were down, as were the portable toilets. Even the Marquee was rolled up and packed away.

Tools and machines thrown aside by the tornado were back and ready for moving again. But where were they going? Were they leaving the island?

And Querciabella's Tree of Life. It stood as strong and proud as ever. Around it, two men erected a barrier, with banners attached saying:

No Entry. This is a Protected Area.

They dug a hole for a signpost with the words:

THIS IS A TREE PROTECTION AREA.   KEEP OUT.

"Yippee, Gagzy! Mum was right! Querciabella's Tree of Life is saved!" Gogzy could barely contain her excitement.

"It's brill, Gogzy. Isn't it amazing? Whitewave told us to seek the advice of the mum, and now here we are, looking at the result."

"It's amazing, Gagzy. And look what's going on over there, beside the turret. It's Officer Sophia."

The girls waved to her, and she waved back.

"She's not coming over to talk to us, Gogzy. Look who she's with."

"It's the lady with the glossy, red lipstick."

"And look what's lying on the ground beside them."

"It's the ten bags of poisoned stuff, Gagzy. And there are two men putting them into a barrow and wheeling it away. They're getting rid of the poison stuff, just as mum said they would. Hip! Hip! Hurray! I say!"

"Me too, Gogzy."

"And look again! Look at her, the lady with the glossy, red lipstick, Gagzy… She's staring right at us. Look at her face.

That is an angry face! I bet she knows we told mum all about the bags of poison and how she left us trapped inside those caves, inside the dungeons.

I bet she wants to scream some of that angry face at us, but she's too scared to do it, because Sophia is taking her away by the arm."

"And quite right too, Gogzy. She'll have to explain herself now.

But what's happening with all the people and the workers gathered."

"Maybe they've decided to leave the island, Gagzy. The Tree of Life has been saved. And the poison stuff has been discovered, so the otters and the beavers are safe too. They can't harm them."

"But remember what the man in the blue dungarees told us, Gogzy. He said they were moving to a different part of the island."

"I see him, Gagzy… Over there, beside the dumper trucks and the two big feller buncher machines. Let's go and ask him what's happening. If we find out more, we should tell Querciabella any news we can get."

They ran across the clearing to talk to the man in the blue dungarees.

"Ahah!", he exclaimed.

"So, you're back again. Maybe you should ask mum and dad to get you a house on the island."

"No, we just like visiting." Gagzy told him.

"But what's happening now? Are you leaving, with all your stuff gathered here? Are you leaving the island?"

"Oh, no, no, no! The boss would have none of that. There's work still to be done. We're moving to the woodlands and nearer to the sea on that side of the island. Didn't I tell you? We'll chop down some trees and build a resort in the woods close to the white sandy beach there. We'll pitch the tents nearby. I've no doubt we'll be seeing you girls over there too.

Start moving, guys." He called out to the workers.

"But wait!" Gogzy yelped.

"We told you before. There's something bad in the woods, and not just that, there are people living there."

"No, no, no. That's all been checked. No one lives in the woods. We must get a move on now. Start moving, guys." He said again.

The fleet of trucks, and the big lorry began moving towards the forest trees.

"Quickly, Gogzy. Let's see if we can find Querciabella. We must tell her about this."

"What should we do, Gagzy? We don't have the hieroglyph she told us about. We can't get inside the Tree of Life without that."

"Let's just try knocking, same as Misnich and the Gnomes did."

They stood beside the oak tree.

"You do the knocking, Gogzy. You've always been good at getting inside mystery trees. Just five knocks, same as Misnich did."

"Ok, Gagzy."

Knock… Knock… Knock… Knock… Knock…

Gogzy tapped her knuckles five times on the bark of the tree.

"Welcome, Gogzy and Gagzy.", came Querciabella's reply.

She knew who was there.

"Enter the Tree of Life where you see the light on the bark. Walk into it as though it was an open door."

The sisters did as they were bid and passed through to find Querciabella seated by the fireside.

"I've been expecting you. Whitewave told me you have some things to tell me."

"Wow! How did she know?", exclaimed Gogzy.

"Oops, I forgot. Whitewave knows things before they happen."

"So, tell me your news.", said Querciabella.

"Everything has changed, Querciabella.", said Gagzy.

"The Tree of Life is safe, and it's protected. None of our *'big folk'* can touch it now.

"Misnich told me how your protest had succeeded. We are forever in your debt, Gagzy and Gogzy."

"And Whitewave's river is safe too.", said Gogzy.

"We wanted to tell her, but we couldn't find her. It's not just the Tree of Life, which is protected, but the animals who live on the riverbanks… They too are protected."

"Whitewave is in the deep sea of Eilean to think on what is to come, Gagzy and Gogzy. She has foreseen troublesome times ahead, troubles which may be too much for us. She has seen the rise of the Dark Elemental. She has foreseen Ignis rise in fury."

"I knew it!", exclaimed Gogzy.

"It's the *'big folk'*, the developers, Querciabella.

They've stopped making a golf course and building houses. They're moving all their stuff, all their tents and trucks, they're moving them near to the forest and they're going to chop down trees there and build a holiday camp near the sea on the other side of Moreau Island."

"And we told them there is something bad in the forest, and that people live there, but they just ignored us. We're just kids to them, and I don't think they know that Gnomes live in the forest.", said Gagzy.

The look on Querciabella's face changed from smiling to serious.

"This is grave news you bring to me, Gagzy and Gogzy. It explains Whitewave's foresight of what is to come. The arrival of *'big folk'* in large numbers will disturb the Dark Elemental.

But it will also cause the Gnome clans to rise in defence of their homes. I must go into the forest and consult with the Gnomes. I must tell them the battle to come is not with the *'big folk'*. The greatest danger will come from Ignis, the Dark Elemental. He is the greatest destroyer.

Perhaps you should return home, Gagzy and Gogzy, to be safe."

"Will there be a **real** battle Querciabella?", Gogzy asked, alarmed.

"Only with the Dark Elemental. You may **see** it and be unharmed. But if he comes as a fiery Force of Nature, you must keep a safe distance. You must stay away from fire. You will know that fire can touch you and it can harm you.

For now, you may remain here within the safety of the Tree of Life. Should you decide to leave, walk through the bark of the tree as though it wasn't there. And if you wish to return later, here is the Hieroglyph I promised. I will be in the forest with the Gnomes and Pixies."

With the sharp nail on her index finger, Querciabella drew the image of an oak tree with seven branches, three on the left side of the trunk, and four on the right side.

"Use your own finger, either of you, to outline this image on the outside bark of my tree. The image will glow, and a light will shine on the bark, so you may enter. Thank you again, Gagzy and Gogzy."

With those words, Querciabella vanished.

"Wow! Vanishing visions!", exclaimed Gagzy.

"She's skedaddled again. How did she do that? Where did she go, Gogzy?"

"To the forest to talk to the Gnomes… The *'big folk'* won't be there yet. All their trucks and tents and everything will slow them down.

So, Querciabella has probably gone to tell the Gnomes that they, the *'big folk'*, are on their way and that Ignis, the Dark Elemental, is the greatest danger.

As soon as the *'big folk'* arrive he'll be disturbed from his lair, and he'll be furious, Gagzy. I'm glad Querciabella gave us the secret hieroglyph. I feel safer now we have it."

"Me too, Gogzy."

"What should we do now, Gagzy?"

"Let's see what's going on outside. And I think we should walk over to the woods and see if anything has started to happen. Querciabella said we can see what's going on."

"Yes, Gagzy, but she said we must stay away from fire. If the Dark Elemental is there as a Force of Nature, that's dangerous for us. Fire can touch us."

"We'll keep well away from it, Gogzy. We'll watch from a distance."

As was her way, Gagzy couldn't resist getting close to the action.

"Will we be safe, Gagzy?" Gogzy asked in her squeaky voice, the one that came out when she was a bit scared about what might be coming next.

"Yes. We'll be ok. If there's anything fiery, we just stay away from it. Ok? We'll find a safe place to hide."

"Ok, Gagzy."

Gogzy trusted her sister, even though she knew she was always too quick to rush into the middle of the scary stuff.

They did as Querciabella told them and walked through the bark of the tree as though it wasn't there.

They broke into a running pace till they saw the *'big folk'* and their trucks in the distance, about to enter a woodland pathway.

"We should slow down, Gogzy. We'll find our own place to hide.

The workers and all their stuff will need to find an open space for all their things.

I see some big sycamore trees. We can walk through them and hide behind their thick trunks."

They entered safe cover to hear a weird sound.

"What's that noise, Gagzy?", Gogzy whispered.

"I know what it sounds like Gogzy. It makes no sense, but it sounds like a baby crying, but louder than a baby. Let's see if we can find where it's coming from."

They tip-toed through shadowy spaces between sycamore trees, following the sound, till they saw light in the distance.

Reaching it, they hid behind a thick trunk and peeped around its edge.

They were close to a forest clearing with an estuary where the river met the sea. In the clearing was a lagoon, a pool, with white sand separating it from the estuary.

But there was much more, and they stared at the scene. The sight which met their eyes was one only their psychic eyes could see.

On one side of the lagoon were Gnomes in large numbers, all wearing clan kilts and carrying buckets. It was a gathering of both male and female Gnomes.

Among them were McNubby, McKnobbly, and McKnuckly, with girlfriends also wearing clan kilts and carrying buckets.

On the other side of the lagoon were troupes of Pixies in large numbers, carrying pails.

Misnich led one troupe, and even the little Princess Shailagh and other Pixettes were helpers, filling their tiny pails with Eilean's white sands.

Between these two groups, with her back to the sisters, Querciabella held Cumhachd in her right hand.

And at the edge of the lagoon, in shallow water, Ignis the Dark Elemental, raised his massive body, in the shape of a giant, black, and yellow-spotted salamander.

He was in his lair, the forest lagoon, a place where he was born at the dawn of antiquity.

This was where he slept in a deep burrow on the edge of the pool.

But he was aroused, awakened, like a giant sloth from its slumber, by the *'big folk'*.

They had started to make camp in a nearby forest glade. They were noisy, calling to each other, laughing and banging poles into the ground for their tents.

They didn't know the giant salamander was close, or that it was they who had disturbed him from his sleep.

Ignis raised and heaved his long body, crawling along edge of the lagoon, nearer to the glade where the *'big folk'* were making all the noise.

He swayed from side to side as he moved, angry at the intruders.

The sisters peeped, watching everything from a safe distance, still hiding behind sycamore trees.

They stared in awe at what they saw.

"Look at him, Gagzy. Ignis is gigantic. He is moving. He's a Brobdingnagian monster. He's so big, big, big! He's as big as a train, all covered in yellow spots, and sparks flying off him. He's on fire! Are we too close?"

"We're ok here, Gogzy. No one sees us."

"I see Princess Shailagh, Gagzy. She's tiny, in her bare feet, and she's filling her pail with sand. There's an army of Pixies and Pixettes, all with pails and spades!"

"I see them, Gogzy, and the Gnomes we met, they're filling big buckets with mud, sand, and water.

They're with their girlfriends. And look closely, Gogzy. Their girlfriends aren't wearing shoes, and they don't have hairy feet!"

"Yikes! Thank goodness!", exclaimed Gogzy.

Ignis was on fire, a flaming beast, as he moved. The weird sound of a baby crying was coming from **his** mouth. But Ignis was not a baby!

He was aroused and angry... In a raging fury at the arrival of those *'big folk'*.

He released his fury by snorting fireballs from flaring nostrils...

Huge, flaming fireballs shot out of those nostrils. They rolled into the forest glade... a warning to the *'big folk'* to go away!

And Ignis had company. His servants arrived... A flock of screaming howlers hovered and fluttered around him. They had thick skin which was rough and gnarled.

Their wings had no feathers, and their heads were hawkish with sharp, pointed beaks.

The *'big folk'* in the nearby forest glade had no sight of the salamander, but some saw the blast of fireballs roll through the glade.

The sight and roaring sound of blazing balls forced them to stop setting up camp. Many ran for cover and hid in trees, terrified, and out of sight.

But others were too busy. They saw nothing. They carried on working, adding to the fury of Ignis. He snorted more burning balls towards the sounds of thumping and banging coming from the glade.

Querciabella gave orders.

"Ignis must be stopped. He might start a forest fire! So, douse his fire, Clan Mcknuckly." She called.

"Fill your buckets with sand, mud, and water. Douse his flaming body with the mixture."

"Fill your pails, Pixies."

She whispered in the Pixie tongue. Even amid all the noise and bustle, the Pixies heard her silent whispers.

"Fill your pails with white sand. Douse the tongues of fire with the white sands of Eilean."

Hundreds of Pixies raced to do their jobs.

"Change his course, Clan McNubby.", she called.

"Drive him into the estuary. Whitewave and Anemone are ready to challenge him. Drive him into the river and the sea."

"More mud and sand, Clan McKnobbly. Fill your buckets. Drench him in sodden mud and sand."

But still, Ignis moved, and still his flames burned.

"Which way is he going, Gagzy? Is he coming our way?"

Gogzy didn't watch. She had looked away. She felt safer behind the tree, clinging to its thick trunk.

"What's all the screaming? Are the *'big folk'* running away?"

"I don't know, but we're ok, hiding behind these sycamore trees, Gogzy.

The Pixies and Gnomes are forcing him to move along the river where it flows into the sea. And the screaming is coming from the screaming howlers. They're flying all around him. Come, don't worry. No one knows we're here. Look round the trunk. Do you see those screaming howlers?"

"I see them. They're much worse than seagulls screaming in my ears."

"And do you see Ignis? He's heading for deeper water to shake off all the mud and sand."

"I see him Gagzy. And look at the giant waves!"

The weight of Eilean sand and mud forced Ignis to crawl across the estuary, into the sea, to wash it away, his fire unabated.

But he was unprepared for Whitewave and Anemone.

A gentle breeze turned suddenly into a rogue storm and mighty waves of the Eilean Sea lashed and engulfed him.

The two feminine Forces of Nature produced a swollen sea, amid a storm of such power, Ignis was beaten.

In his chosen form as a salamander, he could not match the power of Anemone and Whitewave.

Out of Anemone's tempest came a whirlwind.

And in the Eilean Sea, Whitewave's clashing currents induced a maelstrom, a giant whirlpool of oceanic power.

Anemone spun the salamander's flaming body in the whirling wind as Whitewave sucked him into the titanic maelstrom.

The sisters remembered Anemone's words of mystery…

'The wind blows as it will in any dimension'.

As a salamander ignis was defeated in the Eilean Sea.

His one chance of escape was to change shape.

There was no escape on land, in river or in sea, so, he thrust himself upwards, and out of the swirling whirlpool, like the phoenix, he became airborne, an enormous bird, its wings aflame with gold and scarlet tongues of fire.

The screaming howlers could not follow into the bright sunlight. They hid in the shadows of the trees, still screaming as they did so.

With Ignis out of reach, Querciabella took immediate action.

"Cumhachd, cuidich." She said the words quietly as she raised Cumhachd skywards.

From their hiding place behind the sycamore trees, Gagzy and Gogzy watched in awe as the flaming clash of two fearsome birds unfolded.

"Gogzy, Cumhachd is an eagle again. She's bigger than the fiery bird. She's chasing him.

See how she soars high on the wind. Wow! Now she's stooping. She's diving! She is bulleting downwards towards Ignis, towards the giant bird with wings of fire!"

"I see it, Gagzy. She's caught him in mid-air. Her talons have grabbed him, and the two ginormous birds are rolling across the sky in a blazing battle. Who's going to win?"

They must wait to find out because some of the screaming howlers had spotted the girls and were heading towards them.

"Run, Gagzy! Quickly, run!"

Gogzy sprinted from her hiding place and Gagzy followed, but the howlers were used to flying in shadowy places. They winged through the trees with ease and surrounded the sisters, screaming ear-piercing screeches.

Their strident screams hurt the girls' ears.

Gogzy closed her eyelids to hide their ghastly faces, with hawkish, piercing eyes and sharp, beaky noses.

"Help, Gagzy! It's too much for me!"

She covered her ears to block the screams.

They were in a thicket of trees, not far from the edge of the woodland. They might soon be out of there.

Gagzy didn't panic. She remembered Querciabella's advice.

'If a screaming howler chases you, reply only by saying quietly, my name…
Querciabella…

They will bullet into the sky, screaming and howling as they go. My name alone will throw them into a mighty muddle.'

It was good advice.

"It's ok, Gogzy." She told her sister.

"Remember what Querciabella told us."

And Gagzy said the word quietly, without panic in her voice.

Querciabella…"

Instantly, the howlers panicked in disarray. They flew skywards, screaming and bumping into each other as they met the bright sunlight which they hated.

Their howling screams grew louder… So loud the *'big folk'* in the forest glade below heard those screams. Their eyes searched the sky for a sight of the howlers.

They heard the ear-piercing sounds, but who or what was doing the screaming? They saw no screamers.

The *'big folk'* did not have the *'sight'* to see them.

But they did see a ball of fire, burning in flames of gold and scarlet, falling, till it splashed into the sea below and was extinguished. The flames of the Phoenix bird were quenched, snuffed out by the waters of the Eilean estuary.

The *'big folk'* had not seen the battle between Cumhachd and the Phoenix bird. They saw only the flames of the defeated bird as it fell.

It was all too much for those *'big folk'*.

They hadn't seen the screaming howlers, but what they **had** seen on Moreau Island had become too much for them.

They had seen their own workers run away in terror of ghostly phantoms.

They saw the weird fate of their new golf course, where the holes re-filled themselves every night…

And the mighty Marquee tent which they erected… It collapsed every night.

Their plan to re-shape the river was stopped by freak weather… Scuppered by a tornado!

Their efforts to remove an oak tree were foiled by a couple of kids.

They had seen fireballs roll across the forest glade. How was it possible?

Where had they come from?

They heard the hideous screams of unseen howlers.

And they saw the shape of burning flames fall from the sky. Where had those flames come from?

It was time to pack up and leave the haunted island. Those developers could take no more. Their workers were in terror of what might come next.

But it wasn't over yet for Gagzy and Gogzy.

The mention of Querciabella's name was enough to scatter the screaming howlers.

But was worse still to come?

The Phoenix bird was defeated, but the spirit of the Dark Elemental had reshaped himself again. He was out of his lair, out of the lagoon, and he was prowling.

Ignis was in the woods.

He was there in the shape of a lion with a fiery mane, burning in red and white flames which surrounded his face and neck. He was a fearsome sight to behold, weaving through woodland trees, while those high flames licked the tree trunks as he passed.

Had he picked up the scent of Gagzy and Gogzy?

Relieved to be free of the screaming howlers, Gogzy was calm.

She whispered, not knowing what might be nearby.

"What's that bright light moving through the trees, Gagzy? Do you see it? Do you see how it's swerving around each tree as it moves? Is it following us?"

"I see it.", Gagzy gulped.

"I think it's Ignis, Gogzy. He's in the shape of a lion, and his head is on fire. The big flames around him are brushing the sides of the trees! I hope he hasn't sniffed our scent. He's sniffing the ground as he moves."

Gogzy's calmness deserted her.

"Oh no!", she yelled.

"He's sniffing the ground. He might be hungry, Gagzy. He might be hungry after his long sleep! He might be starving! He might…"

Gogzy stopped herself. She couldn't say the words… *'He might eat us!'*

"Oh no! He could start a forest fire! And we're in here, Gagzy!", she screamed.

Suddenly, a thunderous roar resounded through the woods.

It had come from the stalker. And the stalker was Ignis!

"Run, Gogzy. Get out of the woods. Remember what Querciabella told us. He can't touch us, and he can't bite you. He won't eat us. He's not a real lion! He's a spirit from another dimension!"

"But Gagzy! He's also a Force of Nature! He might start a forest fire!"

They bolted, leaving the woods behind them, they ran like they were in a sprint race, not daring to look back till they saw some *'big folk'* ahead who had left the forest glade.

They chased after them.

When they did look back there was no sign of Ignis.

And relief flooded through their veins when Gugzy bounded up to them with his usual licking, jumping and wanting to play.

The *'big folk'* were heading for the jetty and the cargo boat which was moored there. They were leaving the island for good.

The man with the Rottweiler spoke to them.

"We're leaving.", he told them.

"Coming here has been a big mistake.

I don't suppose you would like a dog, would you? Would you like to keep Gugzy. You're made for each other, and he's been pining for you two."

The sisters' eyes lit up and they gasped at the offer.

"We're moving on to another project." He told them.

"I will be too busy to give Gugzy the time he needs.

If you say yes, I'll leave my phone number with you, just in case your mum and dad aren't keen on the idea. But he loves you two. Trust me, he does."

"Yes! Yes! Yes!", The sisters yelled in unison, and the man with the Rottweiler passed Gugzy on his leash to Gagzy, with a note of his phone number, his name, and the name of Gugzy's vet.

"I hope you get to keep him. All the very best to you, girls."

And the man with the Rottweiler headed off with the others to board the cargo boat.

"Yipee!", exclaimed Gogzy.

"We love you, too, Gugzy!", exclaimed Gagzy, as he jumped and licked her cheeks.

"And now we're a threesome… Gagzy, Gogzy, and Gugzy!"

"What now, Gagzy. Should we head off home?"

"Not yet, Gogzy. We have the secret hieroglyph. Let's go into Querciabella's house. If she isn't there, we can wait for her. And look, it's raining, it's bucketing down. Quickly… To the Tree of Life… Come on, Gugzy."

They arrived at the oak tree.

"Can you do the hieroglyph, Gogzy? Can you draw it with your fingertip?"

Gogzy touched the bark of the tree trunk and made the sign of the secret hieroglyph…

As her finger traced the shape, a glowing image appeared. It was the image of an oak tree with three branches on the left side and four on the right side.

"Wow, Gagzy. It works!"

They entered, walking through the glowing bark like it was an open door.

"We can forget about Ignis now, Gogzy. Ignis can't follow us. He can't enter the Tree of Life."

Inside they sat beside the warm fire and waited for Querciabella, while Gugzy curled up snugly on the floor.

When she arrived later, Querciabella carried Cumhachd in her right hand.

She told the sisters how Anemone and Whitewave sent a long and heavy fall of rain across the woodland to douse the flames on trees where Ignis had prowled. There was no forest fire.

And she told the girls the battle with Ignis was over.

She, the Gnomes, and the Pixies found him pacing and scratching around the glade, checking the *'big folk'* were gone.

When he was sure they had left, he returned quietly to his lair, a burrow on the edge of the lagoon, where he would sleep a long sleep if he was left undisturbed.

"You will always be welcome here in the Tree of Life, Gagzy and Gogzy, and you too, Gugzy.", she smiled as Gugzy raised his head in attention.

"And you know the secret hieroglyph. It will remain your secret. So, I bid you farewell."

"It's been so wonderful to meet you and your friends, Querciabella. We will miss you.", said Gagzy.

"Bye, bye.", said Gogzy.

"I would love to give you a big hug, but I haven't forgotten. We're in different dimensions."

Querciabella smiled and the sisters took their leave to return home, where mum and dad gave them the amazing news… They were allowed to keep Gugzy.

Gagzy, Gogzy, and Gugzy were an item, a team.

From that day on, they were inseparable besties.